THE CASE OF THE DEAD JURORS

Also by Rod Sterling

A Tony and Mindy Mystery
The Traffic Stoppers Case
The Case of the Yearbook Murders
Murder at Hessian's Bridge
The Case of the Dead Jurors

Short Stories
In the Thick of Things

THE CASE OF THE DEAD JURORS

A Tony and Mindy Mystery

By

Rod Sterling

HOLLISTON, MASSACHUSETTS

THE CASE OF THE DEAD JURORS
Copyright © 2017 by Rod Sterling

This book is a work of fiction. Names, characters, places and incidents are products of the author's imagination or are used fictitiously. Any resemblance to actual events, locations or persons, living or deceased, is entirely coincidental.

Printed and bound in the United States. All rights reserved. No part of this book may be reproduced or transmitted in any form or by any means, electronic or mechanical, including photocopying, recording, or by an information storage and retrieval system—except by a reviewer who may quote brief passages in a review to be printed in a magazine, newspaper, or on the Web—without the express written consent of Silver Leaf Books, LLC.

The Silver Leaf Books logo is a registered trademarks of Silver Leaf Books, LLC.

All Silver Leaf Books characters, character names, and the distinctive likeness thereof are trademarks of Silver Leaf Books, LLC.

Cover Art by Aveliya.

First printing November 2017
10 9 8 7 6 5 4 3 2 1

ISBN # 1-60975-201-5
ISBN-13 # 978-1-60975-201-9
LCCN # 2017950968

Silver Leaf Books, LLC
P.O. Box 6460
Holliston, MA 01746
+1-888-823-6450

Visit our web site at www.SilverLeafBooks.com

Gratefully...

I'm told that Harriet Beecher Stowe had eight children underfoot while she wrote longhand on foolscap. Did she have a group to review and critique her stuff? Did Mark Twain? Robert Louis Stevenson? What about Poe, Doyle or O.Henry?

I have been fortunate enough to have the Central Virginia chapter of Sisters in Crime. (Myself and one other guy are the only misters.)

When they like something, they say so. When they don't like, they say so. I probably incorporate 90% of their suggestions into the final work. I thank them one and all.

Frances Aylor, Jim Bacon, Susan Campbell, Kate Cooke (former member), Mary Dutta, Susan Edwards, Marilyn Mattys, Kathleen Mix, Rosemary Stevens, Mary Miley Theobald (group moderator), Sandie Warwick, and Heather Weidner.

I also want to thank Frances Burch for her contributions in two earlier groups.

WHO'S WHO

HARRY CASSETTI: He didn't do it but smirked at the judge and got the electric chair.

THE JUDGES: Malcolm Willcox gave the death penalty, Endicott Huber tried to protect the system.

THE LAWYERS: Lou Notella prosecuting attorney went on to bigger things; but the reverse was true for defense attorney Bob Haines.

THE JURORS: Malina Bankowski, Marcy Cavanagh, Elizabeth Collins, Theresa Froumy, Susan Ganley, Kathleen Geiger, Edward Gleason, Norman Jackson, Charlie Jenkins, Carol McKelvey, Donald Nagle, and Andy Panzavecchia.

BRENDAN CAVANAGH: His wife, Marcy, drowned, and he thought it was fishy.

TONY DONOHOO: Private Eye extraordinaire. Cavanagh hired him to find out what happened.

MINDY McCALL: Tony's girl Friday and Tony's girl.

THAIS HAINES: Wife of defense attorney Bob Haines. She was up for the familiar face award.

DOLLY AND FRANK DONOHOO: Tony's brother and wife were always ready to lend a hand.

PATRICIA AND AL ZIPOLI: Summertime neighbors of the Cavanaghs - They had family secrets.

HARRY CASSETTI JR.: He was serving in Korea

STEPHEN KILMURRAY: (nee Cassetti) Another son. He hated and was ashamed of his father.

PATRICK GANLEY: He picked potato salad over protecting his wife.

CHARLOTTE AND PETER ROSSI: They won't even have to go to Reno.

EUSTACE RENAHAN: His Cadillac days are over.

TONI ANN GLEASON: Her husband kept her in the dark.

THE CASE OF THE
DEAD JURORS

ONE

Saturday, October 10, 1953, 12:45 P.M.

The detective game was in the dump. Not a single divorce lawyer referral in two months. No skip tracers to find. Nothing. Cash flow was down to a trickle. Tony Donohoo sat at the bar of the Yellow Front Saloon chewing on a hamburger and washing it down with a bottle of Schlitz.

"Whatsamatta, Tony? You don't look happy," observed Frankie from behind the bar. Frankie was Tony's older brother.

"I got nothin' goin', Frankie. Bank account is near empty. If you need somebody a couple of nights behind the stick, give me a yell. I could use the money. And I still owe you a hundred from last week." Tony was referring to the sum he had borrowed from his brother, Frankie, to finance the annual pilgrimage to New England that Mindy insisted upon to see the fall foliage each year in the first week of October. All of Vermont and the rest of New England were bathed in glorious gold, orange and red. Mindy, his longtime girl friend and detective operative, was also a commercial free-lance photographer. The first week of October was hog heaven to a photographer. She made the trip bedecked with camera bags and a dozen rolls of film. They had gotten an early start on Friday afternoon in Mindy's Kelly green '51 Ford convertible. The balmy weather permitted the entire trip to be with the top down. They checked into a small country inn in Arlington. To satisfy the blue-nosed Vermont innkeeper, Mindy spun her Hackensack High class ring around to appear as a plain gold wedding band. This enabled Tony to sign the register "Mr. and Mrs. Anthony Donohoo, of Hackensack, New Jersey." The merchants and townspeople varied their normal caustic attitudes and distrust of visitors just a bit in anticipation of the short lived economic boom brought on by the dazzling array the forests of Sugar Maple, Ash, Beech, and Yellow Birch displayed with the change of season.

Saturday was spent photographing covered bridges, dynamic flora, and attending overpriced church sales with stalls under tents selling goods at 300% of what the locals would pay, if they were to buy the stuff at all. Tony actually enjoyed the crustiness of the natives. That evening, Tony and Mindy had a luxurious dinner of clam chowder and braised pork at the Four chimneys Inn in Rutland.

"Don't worry about the C-note, Tony. I know you're good for it," Frankie said.

It's good to have a big brother, thought Tony, *even if he's smaller.*

Frankie moved down the bar to address a man that was not a regular. He had walked in and was looking over the patrons with a quizzical look on his face. He was in his forties and wore slacks, an open collar shirt and a cardigan. "Can I help you, pal?"

"I'm looking for Tony Donohoo," came the answer.

"That's my little brother," said Frankie with a wide grin. "That's him with the long puss and the hamburger."

"I don't want to disturb your lunch," the man said. "Your receptionist told me you'd be here."

"No, that's all right, take a load off." The man hopped up on the stool next to Tony. "What's on your mind?"

"My name's Brendan Cavanagh. I may want to hire you."

"To do what?"

"It's kind of confidential. Is there some place we can go?"

"We can move to a table, or if you want to wait a couple of minutes, we can go to my office, which is behind that bookcase over there. You want a beer, or somethin'?"

"No, no thanks. I'll wait. Finish your lunch. I'm in no hurry."

* * *

"What's on your mind?" Tony repeated, now seated behind his desk and facing Mr. Cavanagh.

"What's with the secret door?" asked the visitor, smiling.

"It's a throwback to Prohibition. Pop ran a speakeasy in the saloon. The front was all boarded up and the way to get in was by entering the real estate office, into this room, and then passing into the barroom. In those days, you could sell all the booze you wanted just so long as it didn't look like that's what you were doing. Now, what's troubling you?"

"My wife died in a so-called accidental drowning a couple of months ago." Cavanagh's voice broke slightly.

"Sorry to hear that. Why so-called?"

"I have a cabin up on Sunrise Lake in New York State. It's been in the family since my grandparents built it around the turn of the century."

"I know Sunrise Lake. I've been there visiting friends." said Tony.

"We go up on weekends starting in April, and after the summer's over, as late as Thanksgiving.

During the summer, my wife and kids would spend all week there, and I would come up on Friday nights and head back Tuesday mornings. "My wife, Marcy, was a strong swimmer and in the habit of taking a swim in the lake by herself about seven each morning. It woke her up. She'd return full of energy. There's a float anchored out in the lake about fifty yards. It's about ten by ten and buoyed up by a bunch of 55 gallon drums. A couple of teenagers found her body under the float tangled up in the anchor cables." Cavanagh dipped his head. His eyes were tearing.

Tony pulled a bottle of brandy out of his desk. He poured three fingers into a thick water glass with decades of surface scuffing and handed it to Cavanagh. "Drink this."

Cavanagh threw it down in one swig. "Thanks."

"How deep is the water there?" asked Tony, getting back on track.

"About fifteen feet. Anyway the coroner's inquest ruled it an accidental death. I didn't feel too good about that, but there didn't seem to be anything further to do."

"Was she a big woman?

"No, about five-two, 110 pounds."

"Were you at the lake when it happened?"

"No, it was a Thursday...May 28th. I'm an advertising copywriter. I go into the city two or three times a week. I was in my office when I got the call."

"Where do you work?"

"Midtown, off Madison."

"How come you only go in a couple of times a week?"

"I'm not an employee, but an independent contractor. I get paid a percentage of agency revenues derived from what I produce. I do a lot of my work at home."

"And what do you want me to do?"

"There's more." Cavanagh leaned forward in his chair as if he were about to whisper a secret. "This week I was riding the bus into the city. There were two guys sitting right in front of me. I'd seen them many times but didn't know them, if you follow me. Just enough to nod hello. But they seemed well acquainted with each other. They were talking about a mutual acquaintance who had been killed recently in Hackensack. The dead guy, Norman Jackson, was working on his car and had it jacked up. He was under the car and the jack slipped out and he was crushed to death."

"Did you know this Jackson guy?" Tony pulled out his Luckies, offered the pack to Cavanagh, who refused, and then lit his own.

"No. I read about it in the paper a couple of weeks ago, but I didn't know him. Do you remember a murder trial back in '47 for a guy named Harry Cassetti?"

"Yeah, sure. They called him Harry "the Cat" Cassetti. He got the electric chair for killing his wife."

"That's it. Only he didn't do it. There was a lot of circumstantial evidence against him. He was known to beat his wife and the kids. His prints were on the gun. Neighbors had heard him threaten to kill his wife, and a lot more. He routinely cheated on her and was something of a ladies' man. The jury was unsympathetic. Anyway, he was convicted and executed in '48.

"Then last year, another guy was about to be fried, and got religion at the last minute. In confessing his sins to a priest, he admitted being the one who actually killed the Cassetti woman. The priest told him that he had to tell the authorities if he wanted absolution. He did. At first they didn't believe him, or didn't want to, but he came up with facts that were never made public, and the state realized that Harry Cassetti had been wrongfully convicted and executed."

"Okay, I remember that. But how does that tie in with the two guys on the bus."

"One of them reminded the other that Norman Jackson had been one of the jurors on the Cassetti trial."

"Yeah, so what?"

"So was my wife," said Cavanagh.

TWO

"So," said Tony, "you're thinking that two jurors who voted guilty in the Cassetti trial have died by accident a few months apart, and that's too much of a coincidence?"

"Yeah, but both accidents could easily have been deliberately caused. I mean, if one of the jurors died in an airplane crash, a bunch of other people would also be killed. An avenging angel, if there is one, couldn't justify that. Both of these accidents were directed only at former jurors."

"Mr. Cavanagh, I gotta tell you. It's a stretch. Do you know if any other jurors might have also died by accident?"

"No, but I don't know the identity of the other ten jurors. I doubt if Marcy knew any of their names either. Jurors don't get introduced to one another by name. Anyone could ask another, but after five or six years, who would remember? Getting their names is one of the things I was hoping you'd be able to handle."

"Their identities would be sealed. It would take a court order to get their names, and the assignment judge would never sign it with this evidence, if you could call it evidence."

"Are you telling me you won't take the case?"

"Did I say that? I don't think I said that." *Right now I'd take a case chasing skunks off the garage roof if a paycheck came with the job.*

"So you'll take the case?"

Tony produced a form from his desk drawer. "This is my service agreement. I get $300 for a retainer, non-refundable. When, and if, it runs out, I'll let you know. I get $35 a day. If I have to travel, there'll be an additional $20 a day for hotel and meals. Five cents a mile if I leave the county in my car."

Cavanagh had his checkbook out and quickly signed the service agreement after merely glancing at it. When asked, Cavanagh gave his address, home and office phone numbers.

"How many cars do you have?" asked Tony.

"Now we have just one. I sold my wife's car after her death."

"Do you recall the license plate number on her car?"

"Yes, the plate numbers were just one digit apart. Hers was BMS 478 and mine is BMS 479. Why?"

"Routine," answered Tony, making note of the numbers. Tony maintained a license plate number file on 3 x 5 cards in an old Dewey decimal system file cabinet. It contained about 60,000 cards. When an investigation took him or a part-time operative to any location, it was standard practice to write down the plate numbers of all the other cars in the lot on a yellow lined pad, with the place, hour, and date. The sheet would be turned over to the receptionist who would make up a rubber stamp from a kit with the tweezers

that might look like this:
Charlie's Grill
1700 Route 6
Little Ferry NJ
TU 7/14/52 2100

She would stamp the same number of cards as plate numbers and write each number in the upper left hand corner. The card was filed away alpha-numerically. It was not uncommon for there to be six or seven cards on any one plate number. The lists were also filed, but chronologically. When two plate numbers appeared together on two or more lists, especially if at two different locations, it followed they probably knew one another. If two plates both showed up at a local bar and then at a motel sixty miles away, it was a bingo. The file was very helpful in most divorce cases.

"You got a picture of your wife?"

Cavanagh took a wallet sized photograph out of his billfold and handed it to Tony. "What do you want that for?"

"Investigating. Some people may not have known her name but could recognize her."

"What course are you going to take?" asked Cavanagh.

"I make it up as I go along. I'll be in touch."

THREE

Now fat with cash, Tony got to work. A trip to the library topped his list. There he found four items in the newspaper microfiche archives:
 1. The Harry Cassetti trial in 1947
 2. The death row confession clearing Cassetti
 3. The death of Marcy Cavanagh
 4. The death of Norman Jackson

Articles on the Angela Cassetti murder told Tony the Cassettis had two sons, Harry Jr., 18, and Steven, 17. At the time of the murder, both boys were away working as summer camp counselors at Camp No-be-bo-sco, near Morristown. Harry's story was he came home and found his wife's body in the bedroom. She'd been shot in the chest, and a .32 revolver was lying on the floor. It was Harry's gun. When he came in, he'd picked it up without thinking, but didn't disturb anything else. He called the police. The prosecutor portrayed Harry as a womanizer who had been heard by neighbors to threaten his wife's life. He once was charged in the Teaneck Municipal Court of assaulting her and was given a fine, but no jail time. A parade of witnesses gave testimony damning to Harry. The defense attorney, Robert Anton Haines, had little to go on and was unable to sway the jury in Cassetti's favor. The jury, which deliberated overnight while sequestered in a local hotel as guests of Bergen County, returned a guilty verdict of murder in the first degree to Superior Court Judge Malcolm Willcox. Cassetti was sentenced to die in the electric chair and in June, 1948, the sentence was carried out.

A November 1952 headline read:

"BACKA'" RUDA CONFESSES: CASSETTI WAS INNOCENT

Carlo "Backa" Ruda, due for execution in a few days for the mob hit of Carmine Bongiovanni, confessed to the 1947 murder of Angela Cassetti at her home in Teaneck. Her husband, Harry Cassetti, had been executed for the murder in 1948. Ruda had a lengthy criminal record for armed robbery, burglary, assault with a deadly weapon and felony murder. To grant final absolution before execution, Ruda's priest encouraged him to admit he murdered Mrs. Cassetti. The authorities were reluctant to believe him until he provided details that had never been published. Most notably, he described a slip that she wore was pink with an embroidered red rose on the breast. According to Ruda, he was burglarizing the house, which he thought was empty, when Mrs. Cassetti surprised him. She was holding a gun. He managed to disarm her and in the process, the gun went off, and she was shot. 'The only time I ever killed a broad,' Ruda said.

The May 30th article on Marcy Cavanagh of Maywood

indicated she died by accidental drowning at Sunrise Lake, New York, at the age of 42. She left a husband, Brendan, and three children.

Norman Jackson, of Hackensack, was killed September 29th while working on the underside of his car. He had jacked it up, but the jack slipped and the car crushed him. Jackson was 47. He left a wife, Beatrice, who found her husband dead when she returned from shopping.

Tony filled up several pages in his notebook. On one page he wrote:

>CONTACT
>Harry Cassetti Jr. (now 24)
>Steven Cassetti (now 23)
>Cassetti neighbors in 1947
>Defense Attorney Robert Anton Haines
>Judge Malcolm Willcox
>Prosecuting Attorney Louis Notella
>Beatrice Jackson
>Jackson neighbors
>Cavanagh neighbors at Sunrise Lake and in Maywood

The afternoon was running out when Tony left the library. He had a six o'clock date with Mindy and had just about enough time to clean up.

FOUR

Mindy McCall had a lot of female tricks, but one of them wasn't feigning indifference. So when Tony Donohoo swung his dark blue '49 Ford into her apartment house parking lot, she started out to meet him. As he entered the lobby, the staccato of her heels echoed off the marble floors. Tony had often commented that if he got off a ship in Shanghai and heard those sounds, he'd know Mindy was about to appear around a corner. That heel-clicking alone caused a stirring of his manhood.

He watched with appreciation as her shoulder length red hair swung left and right in rhythmic cadence to the swinging of her hips, as she descended the staircase to the first floor. She wore a tan skirt and chocolate-colored sweater that aspired to match the color of her eyes. She walked into Tony's space and adjusted his tie and buttoned his sport coat.

Mindy had selected Tony when she was in the seventh grade. He was then a handsome six footer in senior year and lived just two blocks from the red-haired twelve year old. When the Japanese bombed Pearl Harbor, her first thought was that Tony would be off to war, and by the following summer, he was. As an eighth grader, the teacher gave an assignment for each student to draw the name of a local serviceman out of a hat and write a letter to him. Mindy drew someone else's name and went on a search for the kid who drew Tony's name. It turned out to be a chubby little boy and Mindy bribed him with her lunch to switch names. She wrote Tony throughout the war and he actually answered three times. Tony was unaware that she still had those letters.

On Armistice Day, 1946, the Hackensack High cheering squad, which included Mindy, were assigned to march in the victory parade down Main Street. Directly behind the cheerleaders were assorted veterans, Army, Navy and Marines. Tony and his cousin, Pete Lionetti, marched in their paratrooper olive-drabs bedecked with fruit salad and jump wings. Mindy got herself positioned toward the rear of the cheering squad so Tony had an excellent view of her shapely legs and perfect derrière, while routinely tossing her long red hair to one side and then the other.

She was confident that Tony would take notice, but was not aware that he knew exactly who she was. Mindy was a carbon copy of a sister ten years her elder that Tony had fallen in love with a decade earlier when he was in the seventh grade and the older McCall girl had been a senior in high school. He routinely left for school half an hour earlier than necessary for no other reason than to say hello to the older McCall girl, who would smile sweetly and say hello back as she waited for the bus.

Mindy got up the nerve the following spring to approach

the young, highly decorated veteran and invited him to be her escort at the senior prom. Tony declined the invitation, begging off not because of her, but that he was 23 years old and couldn't possibly attend a high school dance. She was furious at herself, but even at this late date, had never completely forgiven Tony either. Redheads were like elephants - they didn't forget a thing.

However, several weeks later, after graduation, Tony approached her in Whelan's Drug Store and asked her to go to the movies with him. She realized gleefully that her investment in pursuing Tony had paid off. He took her to the Route 303 Drive-in theater just over the state line in Rockland County, New York to see *The Time Of Their Lives* with Abbott and Costello. Coincidentally, the comedy was set in Rockland County. In the darkness, they sat and necked in Tony's '36 Ford coupe and strolled down to the snack bar for hot dogs before the second feature came on. They continued to date without advancing to a formal engagement for what had become six years. Mindy was in no hurry and was confident that any so-called commitment on Tony's part was unnecessary. In her mind, she had nailed him. In his mind also. A white picket fence, motherhood and washing Tony's underwear was in Mindy's future, but all in good time.

On this October night, she purred "How's my big handsome fella?" while turning her face upward to receive a kiss on the lips. As Tony held the car door open for her, his arousal had not yet begun to abate. Ten minutes later, they were seated in the dining room of the Yellow Front Saloon. The dining room was not a room exactly but a large expanse fully open to the barroom. There were about a dozen dining room sets—no two alike—each covered with a red and white checked tablecloth and an empty Chianti bottle holding a candle.

Whoever was scheduled to work the floor hadn't shown up, and Frankie's wife, Dolly, was filling in.

"Hey, Mindy, you look gorgeous as usual," Dolly gushed. "What are you having?"

"Thanks, Dolly. I'll have a Pabst."

"And I'll have a Schlitz," said Tony. "We'll both have the steak sandwich, medium rare," said Tony.

"Hold the fries on mine but I'll have the onion rings," added Mindy.

"So my little sweetheart got the duty tonight. Who didn't make it in?" Tony asked.

"Sheena had a tooth pulled. I don't mind. And cut the sweetheart crap, Tony. I don't need your blarney," Dolly glared over her shoulder in feigned anger as she headed for the kitchen.

Tony had a theory that regardless of what you name a child, what you call him or her is what he or she will become. Name a child Richard and call him Dick, he will wear a crew cut, smoke a pipe and tend to be boring. But call him Rick or Ricky and he will aspire to living off women. One called Richie will be an obsessive sports fan and never quite mature. Nick will be shuffling cards like a Vegas pro and have the eyes of an eagle, but if he'd been Christened Roger, he'd be wearing horn rims by the second grade.

Name a little girl Elizabeth and call her Liz or Lizzie and she will drink anybody under the table. The same child called Beth will be demure and often wear pearls. Betsy will be able to throw a perfect spiral forward pass before going to high school, but if she's called Betty, by sophomore year she will have a pair of knockers the size of honeydews. A little girl called Dolly will never see 5'2" and will be shaped like a Coca-Cola bottle. Frankie's wife was no exception.

"I got a new client today," said Tony and proceeded to fill Mindy in on the details.

"Well, it's certainly possible for two out of twelve people to be killed accidentally, but it is something of a coincidence. What's the plan now?"

"To identify some or all of the other jurors. For all I know maybe some of them died also."

"Is there anything you want me to do?"

"Yeah, I think so."

By seven o'clock they had finished eating and were on the way to their favorite theater, the Route 303 Drive-In to see *House of Wax*. At the ticket booth, Tony received two pairs of 3-D glasses. Vincent Price played the deranged and deformed mad scientist roaming the darkened fog-laden back streets of London, searching for real bodies he could dip in hot wax and display in his museum. Everyone marveled at how accurate his exhibits were, not realizing they were real bodies At the climax, Phyllis Kirk was being lowered into the hot wax vat naked, when she was rescued. At intermission, Tony and Mindy walked to the snack bar for ice cream.

"If the jury records are sealed, how do you propose to find out who they were?" asked Mindy.

"We'll start with the two lawyers and the judge. You can help out. Which one do you want to interview? Maybe one of them can clue us onto one of the jurors. If we can get one name, maybe that one can identify one or more other jurors, unless he or she is dead. If so, and the death was suicide or accidental, that would be three examples and the assignment judge may issue the order to release the jury records. Once is just once. Twice is coincidence, but three times is almost certainly deliberate."

"Aren't the lawyers and the judge bound to secrecy?"

"I think it depends. If one of them met a juror at some later time by chance, I don't think he would be bound to keep that private."

"All right, I'll take the prosecuting attorney," said Mindy. "But here's another thought: How about running an ad in the paper inviting the former jurors to come forth?"

"Now why didn't I think of that?"

* * *

"In the movies," Tony observed on the drive home, "it's always pitch dark in London with fog so thick you can't see twenty feet. I spent six months there before D-Day. Do you know that it doesn't get dark there until about ten o'clock at night? And the fog is not an every night affair. And how could that freaky Vincent Price running around in a cape and top hat with Igor the hunchback ever manage..."

"Shut up, Tony."

FIVE

Monday, October 12, 1953, 8:50 A.M. Chambers of Superior Court Judge Malcolm Willcox

"I've got ten minutes before court. What's on your mind, Mr. Donohoo?"

"Thanks for seeing me, Judge." Tony then went into the coincidence of the two alleged accidental deaths.

"Hardly conclusive. What do you want from me?"

"Suppose there were more deaths among the jurors. How would you feel about breaking the seal of the identities of the remaining jurors? After all, their lives may be in jeopardy."

"It would depend on how the death or deaths occurred. A death by natural causes wouldn't come into it. But even if another suspicious death occurred and it did seem possible, I would only release the names to the police. This is, of course, academic because I don't have the power to break the seal. That would be up to the assignment judge."

"How did you feel about giving the death sentence to what turned out to be an innocent man?"

"An interesting question. Is this off the record? I don't

want to be quoted in the newspaper."

"Just between you and me, Your Honor."

"I was forty-three when I presided over that trial. I had spent fifteen years on the prosecutor's staff and expected to be the next prosecutor. Instead I was appointed as a superior court judge. I was a little full of myself, as are lots of other judges. I made a mistake and it cost someone his life. But I have learned in life to make the best of something bad, and I have become a much better judge as a result. And, I think—and hope—a much better person."

"You could have given him life instead of the chair," Tony reminded him.

"Hell, I could have overruled the jury altogether and found him not guilty. But I believed the jury got it right. There's one more thing, and I'll deny this if you ever repeat it. I've seen you testify in my court a few times, and I think you're a straight shooter. So here goes. When the jury rendered its verdict, the sonofabitch smirked at me. Cassetti smirked at me. And when I re-think my sentencing, I wonder if that had anything to do with the death penalty over life in prison. I don't actually know the answer, but it won't ever happen again. For me it has been a humbling experience. Not to take all the blame, Cassetti wasn't guilty of murder but he sure was guilty of being incredibly stupid to smirk at the man with the power of life or death over him."

"Thanks for your candor, Judge. One more thing and I'll let you go. Has it occurred to you that if there's someone out to take vengeance that your life may also be in danger?"

"Mr. Donohoo, judges may be arrogant, self-centered

and sometimes even power-mad, but not stupid. You bet your sweet ass it occurred to me. Good luck and I hope you're wrong about this."

* * *

"Mr. Notella will see you now, Miss McCall," said the middle aged receptionist flashing a plastic smile. Louis Notella had been an assistant prosecutor, but he headed up the prosecution at the Cassetti trial. He had since been promoted. His office in the county courthouse was the largest in the prosecution department but not excessively large. It was well furnished but not expensively so. There was the usual law office array of certificates from college, law school and professional milestones. On his cluttered desk was a framed photograph of his wife and four children.

Notella was slightly overweight, with a lopsided smile and curly black hair flecked with gray.

"Good morning, Miss McCall. Please take a seat and tell me how I can help you, or are you here to help me? Either way, it's my pleasure."

Mindy presented her credentials and explained the coincidence of the two alleged accident victims.

"There were ten other people on that jury. We want to know who they were. With only two, it's a bit of a reach to go before the assignment judge and ask for their names, but perhaps with three or four accidental deaths, it could be done. Those still living could be at risk. And if so, I think that risk extends to you, defense attorney Haines, and Judge

Willcox."

"Okay, I see where you're going with this. I'm in sympathy with your objective. And I must admit I'll be on the alert. It's an unusual coincidence, and I'm a skeptic about coincidences. But all that being said, I'm required to keep those names confidential. Jurors are entitled to their privacy."

"Louis no-tella nobody, is that it?" said Mindy in her best *Life With Luigi* accent.

Notella's face morphed into a genuine ear-to-ear grin. "Miss McCall, the first time I heard that, I rolled over, kicked the slats out of my crib and soiled my diaper. But if there's anything else I can do for you, please don't hesitate to let me know. I must admit this shouldn't be dismissed out of hand until more is known. I wish you well. Are you planning on warning Judge Willcox and Bob Haines?"

"My boss, Tony Donohoo is meeting with both of them."

"Judge Willcox is the one responsible for the death penalty, not the jurors. So he seems a likely target for someone avenging the death. Haines tried to get Cassetti off so he probably wouldn't be a candidate for murder. He also was a victim of sorts."

"How so," asked Mindy.

"Haines was up for a superior court judgeship at the time of the trial. He was a shoo-in to be named in '48 or '49. Losing the case was a setback. Then when it turned out Cassetti was not guilty, he was pretty much removed as a judicial candidate. He's pretty bitter about it."

"How exactly does someone become a judge anyway?"

"He's appointed by the governor. But there's a lot of political footsie in play before it gets to the governor's desk. Governor Driscoll is a Republican and so is Haines, of course."

"Thanks for your time, Mr. Notella. You've been helpful. If the need arises, may I call on you again."

"It will be my pleasure. By the way, do you ever go into O'Neill's Bar and Grill over on Passaic Street? They have a real nice happy hour there. You ought to try it sometimes."

* * *

"Robert Anton Haines, Attorney at Law: Rm 206" was written in little white plastic letters fitted into black felt grooves in a glass enclosed case in the lobby. Tony had called first, and Haines said he could talk for a few minutes during lunch hour. Tony guessed the elevator was the building's original from around 1920. It had an open shaft and an expanding gate instead of sliding doors.

He entered the outer office to find the secretary/receptionist desk empty. The furniture was on the dingy side, and the office could use a good cleaning.

"Come through," called a voice. Tony entered to see Haines at his desk and a woman sitting at the side of the desk. If Hackensack High had a girls' football team, she would have been the right tackle. Spread out on the surface was a black barn-shaped lunch box, sandwiches with the crusts cut off, and a pint bottle of chocolate milk. Haines' poorly knotted tie went well with his rumpled brown suit.

One collar point stuck out. Short and stocky at forty, Haines would have only patches of hair over his ears by forty-five. Tony had met Haines a few times and noted the same seemingly confused manner.

"This is my wife, Thais. Thais, meet Tony Donohoo. Hackensack's favorite gumshoe and peeper. What's on your mind, Donohoo?"

"Two of the Cassetti jurors have died in the last few months, supposedly by accident. A Maywood woman named Marcy Cavanagh drowned up at Sunrise Lake in New York State and a Norman Jackson in Hackensack had the jack slip out while he was under the car. I think somebody is very pissed off with how they voted in the trial. My client is the spouse of one of them. I'm trying to find out who the other jurors were."

"You know," Haines responded, "I saw both of those stories in the paper, but never connected them as former jurors on the Cassetti trial. I'm not good with names. Can't help you out. Couldn't tell you if I did remember and I don't."

"If there is a killer, you may be on his list. Have you thought of that?"

"Him?" said Thais, speaking for the first time. "Why would he be on the list? He's the guy that tried to get Cassetti off."

"He's the guy who *failed* to get him off," Tony pointed out.

"Hey, it wasn't my fault that the jury was a bunch of morons," protested Haines.

"I'm not the killer, Haines. He just might be one of those morons. He may also have a different opinion of the quality of your work. If I were you, I'd keep my eyes open. Think twice about staying on your toes.

"You think twice before coming around again, Donohoo. Watch out the door doesn't hit you on the ass on the way out. Vaya con Dios. Get it?"

SIX

As arranged, Tony and Mindy met for lunch at the White Manna Hamburger Stand on River Street in Hackensack. They compared notes about their respective interviews.

"Notella said something funny as I was leaving his office," said Mindy. "He suggested I should go to O'Neill's Bar & Grill for happy hour."

"He was making a move on you."

"I don't think so. I know the difference. He's not a womanizer."

"He didn't look you over?"

"I didn't say that. Of course, he looked. But that's all he did. I get looked over twenty or thirty times a day. I know how to deal with it. And Notella wasn't trying to make it with me."

"So what do you think he meant?"

"I think maybe he was giving me a hint about one of the jurors. Maybe a former juror works there."

* * *

"I'll have a Schlitz, and the lady will have a whiskey

THE CASE OF THE DEAD JURORS • 37

sour," O'Neill's was a typical Jersey gin mill. A gallon jar of hard-boiled eggs was on the back bar alongside another gallon jar of Polish sausages in brine. A Miss Rheingold voting box was at the end of the bar. The liquor bottles were all wiped free of dust and gleamed in the large mirror on the wall. The fifty-ish bartender wore an apron over a white shirt and black tie. His salt-n-pepper hair was combed straight back without a part courtesy of Bryll Cream.

"Sure enough," said the barkeep, placing a basket of pretzels in front of Tony and Mindy.

"What's your name?" asked Tony when the drinks were served.

"Andy."

"Andy O'Neill?"

"No. Dennis O'Neill's the boss. I'm just the day man," said Andy with a shrug and a smile. "Panzavecchia is my last name. Andy Panzavecchia. If that's too much of a mouthful, just call me Andy Panda. That's what everybody calls me."

"Andy, we believe you were a juror on the Cassetti trial back in 1947. We'd like to talk with you about that," Mindy said, taking a stab in the dark. The method was sound because if it hadn't been Andy, he might very well have corrected her with the actual former juror.

Andy's face fell. "Hey, look, I don't wanna talk about that now. I get off in about twenty minutes. I'll talk to you then in private."

Tony and Mindy were on their second round when Andy was relieved. He signaled them to follow him to an empty table at the rear of the tavern. His friendly manner was no longer in evidence.

"Whatdyawanna dig up this muck for? It's over. We made a mistake, but it was an honest mistake. I feel like shit about it. I didn't want to convict the guy. The evidence wasn't for sure, you know? Myself and a few others wouldn't vote guilty the first day. We stayed overnight in a hotel and the next day all the ones who wanted guilty were even more certain, and the rest of us just didn't know. Eventually we all voted guilty. I didn't feel good about it then. I felt worse when the judge gave the poor bastard the chair. Then when it turned out another guy did it, I really felt like crap."

"We're not here to cause you any problems. My name is Tony Donohoo, and this is Mindy McCall. We're private detectives." Tony displayed his shield.

"We've been hired," said Mindy, "to investigate two suspicious deaths of people who were on that jury with you. If it turns out that the deaths were not accidental but murder, then we have two objectives. One is to find the killer, and the other is to warn the other jurors that they may be at risk."

"The problem we're facing right now is that we only know the identity of three of the twelve jurors, and two of them are dead. We can't get the court to open up the record until we have more evidence," explained Tony. "Can you help us identify any of the other jurors?"

"I don't know if I ever knew any of the names. If I did, I don't remember now."

"What can you remember about them?" asked Tony.

"One guy was a car salesman over in Englewood."

"What kind of cars did he sell? Fords, Chevies, what?" asked Mindy.

"No, can't help ya with that. Just an average looking guy. He'd be about my age. Oh yeah, there was a good lookin' broad maybe in her thirties. Not quite in your class, Miss, but a looker all the same. Brunette, she was." Andy accepted one of Tony's Luckies and they both lit up.

"Might this be her?" Tony said offering the photo of Marcy Cavanagh.

"Yeah! That's her. She''s a nice lady. But she was for guilty. But you said the other two jurors were dead. She's dead?"

"She's dead," said Tony.

"Aw, that's a shame, a god damned shame."

SEVEN

Tuesday, October 13, 1953, 10 A.M.

Tony pulled into the lot of British Imports, Ltd. in Englewood. The dealership marketed Jaguars, MGs, Austins, and one or two others. He found the manager's office and flashed his shield, introducing himself as a New Jersey State Detective.

That description was accurate but misleading as almost everyone, including most cops, perceived it to mean New Jersey State Police. Most private investigators were licensed but Tony was commissioned. New Jersey had exactly twelve commissioned detectives. Back in 1871, New Jersey Governor Theodore Fitz Randolph received a couple of death threats. He took them to heart and hired a dozen men to act as bodyguards. The governor sought out men from different police departments reputed to be tough and honest. To sweeten the pot in luring them away from their jobs, he created the commissioned detective. The matter was approved by the state legislature giving them full police powers, including carrying concealed weapons. The commission allowed the detective to operate as a private investigator. Furthermore, the commission was "personalty," which permitted the holder to sell the commission or to pass it down to a son. The recipients were officially known as New Jersey State Detectives.

One such man, a Jersey City detective named Francis Xavier Donohoo, late of County Clare, Ireland, was among the toughest. He didn't carry a blackjack or cosh, but favored a tightly rolled up newspaper., which could be carried openly without attracting attention. A quick straight-on jab in the solar-plexus with the evening paper would bring a strong man to his knees.

The departmental rules that governed permissible off-duty enterprises of a municipal police officer were relaxed for this elite group. So when F. X. Donohoo passed his commission down to F. X. Donohoo Jr. in 1892, there was no obligation to sell Junior's saloon on Main Street in Hackensack, and it continued to operate under the name of Donohoo's Bar and Grill.

In 1915, the saloon and the commission were handed down to F. X. Donohoo III. However, on January 17, 1920, the first day of the Volstead Act enforcement of the prohibition of the manufacture or sale of alcoholic beverages, changes had to be made. In Hackensack, New Jersey, while it was illegal to sell booze, the effect was that an entrepreneur could sell all he wanted just so long as it didn't appear that way. This occurred almost simultaneously with the formation of the New Jersey State Police, which force would now assume the protection of the sitting governor.

No longer on the state's payroll, F. X. Donohoo III's income source was now limited to the profits of the saloon and what little income could be produced as a private investigator. He acquired the next door store front and opened up a sham real estate office. The front of Donohoo's Bar and Grill was boarded up and painted a dull gray to make it appear out of business. A hand-painted sign was affixed to the door: *Gone But Not Forgotten*. The interior of the enterprise remained unchanged but for a "secret" door from the real estate office into the barroom. The door was disguised as a bookcase. It was the worst kept secret in Hackensack, but for the next thirteen years, there was never a day that the saloon was not open for business. Ironically, sales increased by nearly forty percent.

One customer of the speakeasy had been unable to pay a bar bill and F. X. D. III had accepted a half-dozen gallons of glaring yellow paint from him to wipe the slate. When prohibition was repealed on December 5, 1933, the boards were torn off the front of the building and it got a fresh coat of paint—yellow paint. There was just enough to cover only the front of the saloon and the signboard went up reading "Yellow Front Saloon."

When his two sons returned from World War II in 1946, Francis Xavier Donohoo IV (Frankie) was given the saloon, and his younger brother, Anthony, was the recipient of the New Jersey State Detective commission, thereby breaking the F. X. chain.

The concept of commissioned detectives by that time, had little use in modern law enforcement. Keenly aware of this, Tony and the other eleven holders would meet twice a year for lunch to remind each other to keep a low profile. "Don't rock the boat" was an oft-repeated comment at these meetings. The New Jersey State Legislature would not likely revisit the 1871 law if it wasn't creating a problem.

The gentlemanly British manager, conservatively attired in a gray suit and blue and maroon tie, had no doubt he was talking to a police officer.

"How may I help you, sir," he said with a crisp accent.

"I'm looking for an auto salesman who would be about fifty years of age who might have served as a juror in a murder trial back in 1947. Does anyone on your staff come to mind?"

"Well, sir, we have only been operating since 1949. Several members of our sales force are British subjects and none of the others are over forty."

Next stop was the Lincoln-Mercury dealer. The manager couldn't say for sure but steered Tony to one fellow about that age. As Tony approached his cubicle, the fellow smiled and said "Good morning, I'm Dick Brown. You in the market for something new?"

Tony then flashed his shield and gave his intro. "The Cassetti murder trial back in '47—do you remember it?"

"I think so. Wasn't that the guy that got the chair and then they found out somebody else did it?"

"That's the one. Were you on the jury?"

"Me? Why me?"

"Is that a no?"

"Hell, yes, that's a no. Why are you asking?"

"We have reason to believe that those jurors may be in

danger. I know one of them was an Englewood car salesman, but don't know which dealership. The guy would have been in his middle forties back then. About fifty now. How long you been selling cars?

"I started selling Fords back in '31. After I got back from the war, the boss, who owns the Ford agency and the Lincoln-Mercury asked me to switch over. Except for the war years, I been selling cars for over twenty years."

"Can you think of another guy about your age who might have been on that jury?"

"Nothin' comes to mind," said Brown, "and, by the way, I'm only forty-five."

Tony ran into dead ends at the Chevrolet Agency, the Ford, the Oldsmobile-Pontiac, and the Desoto-Plymouth. The last guy followed Tony back to his car. "Have you tried the power steering in the new DeSoto? You can turn the wheel with one finger. Did you see Groucho do it on TV?"

"Thanks, but I'm a Ford guy."

For lunch, he stopped at the Wagon Wheel, an ice cream parlor with a western motif. The Catholic high school, St. Cecilia's, was just around the corner and, a bunch of seniors were in the place. Tony got a burger, fries and a root beer float. Thirty minutes later, at the Buick Agency, he was steered to a salesman named Charlie Jenkins, who fit Andy Panda's description. He offered Tony a seat in his sales cubicle.

After the routine intro, Tony explained what he was investigating.

"Why are you looking for this guy?" Thirty years of cynicism was etched into his face.

"There were twelve jurors. In recent months, two have been killed in what could be accidents or could be something else." Tony took out his Luckies, offered one to Charlie and lit up both with his Zippo. "The court records containing the names of all the jurors are sealed. Assuming these weren't accidents, I have three jobs. One is to find out who those jurors were and if any of the other ten also died suspiciously, the second is to warn them they might be at risk, and the third is to find the killer."

"Maybe I know a guy."

"Yeah? Who?"

"Not so fast. Maybe I should talk to him first. Maybe he's the guy, maybe he ain't."

"Why the mystery?"

"Some people don't appreciate having their names given to the cops."

"I'm not a cop. I'm private. Here's my card. Have him call me."

"What if I just tell him to watch his ass? Won't that do it?"

"No, that won't do it. I'm hoping that he can give me a lead who the other jurors might be."

"So how come the cops aren't working on this? Why you?"

"Because I am the one who got hired by the family of one of the deceased. At this time, the two known deaths occurred in two different jurisdictions—different states, actually—and both were officially declared accidental. Listen, maybe both of them were accidents. I hope so, but two middle aged people—who both served on a jury that found the wrong guy guilty—dying by accident within a couple of months is something of a coincidence. If I don't find any other dead jurors, then I will conclude it was just that—a coincidence. Don't sit on this, Charlie, Okay?"

"Yeah, I hear you."

"So these are the new '54's. Nice. Which one are you using?" Tony said, switching gears.

"That black Roadmaster in the lot," said Charlie.

Tony rose to his feet and turned around as if to leave, then whirled around with the photo of Marcy Cavanagh in his hand. "Did you ever see this woman before?"

Charlie's eyes widened in recognition and then said: "No, I don't know her."

Tony took note of the plate number on the black Roadmaster.

* * *

"Where have you been?" Mindy asked when Tony entered the office.

"I went to almost every auto dealer in Englewood. I think I found the fourth juror but he's playing footsie, saying a friend of his may be the guy. What have you been doin'?"

"I wrote the ad to appear in the paper. Take a look before

I call it in."

> CASSETTI JURORS
> Any jurors in the 1947
> trial of Harry Cassetti
> may be at risk. Friends
> or relatives are also asked
> to come forward. Contact
> Anthony Donohoo
> Investigations.
> HUbbard 8-9740.

"Looks good to me. Run it three days in the *Record*."

"The killer, if there is one, will likely see this ad, too," said Mindy. "I don't look good in black, so watch it."

EIGHT

Wednesday, October 14, 1953, 8:05 P.M.

Charlie and Gertrude Jenkins sat in their small living room in their Englewood bungalow. The rooftop television antenna had been adjusted, and the set showed a clear picture of Groucho Marx on his show *You Bet Your Life*. George Feniman had just announced that the secret word for that night was "clock." As the first two contestants were ushered in, Groucho advised them: "You say the secret word, and the duck comes down and gives you a hundred dollars." Suddenly the TV picture shrank to a white pinpoint in the middle of the screen, and the house was plunged into darkness.

"Sonofabitch! That fuse box again," Charlie moaned. "Where'd you put the flashlight, Gertie?"

"I don't know but I'll try to find a candle."

"Yeah, by the time you do that, the *Late Show* will be on. I'm gonna feel my way to the basement."

"Be careful on those stairs."

"No shit, Gertie?"

Charlie Jenkins groped his way through the kitchen,

opened the basement door and slowly took step by step while grasping the handrail until he felt the cement floor. His hands used the wall to guide him to the fuse box. When he got to the washing machine and laundry tub, he knew the fuse box was immediately beyond. The new fuses were in a box on the top of the fusebox. Charlie took one out, opened the cover door and began to spin the main fuse out of place.

"No shit, Gertie?" were Charlie's last words to his wife of twenty-four years.

* * *

Thursday, October 15th, 1953

"The dumb bastard! What a dumb bastard! All he could figure out was that I had some angle. It never occurred to him that I was simply speaking the truth." Tony spoke as much to himself as to Alice, the receptionist. The afternoon edition of the *Bergen Evening Record* carried a story about Charlie Jenkins being electrocuted in his own basement.

Tony called a friend on the Englewood Police Department and asked to speak to the officer who was first on the scene. That turned out to be one Officer David Bender.

"Yeah, I got there at eight twenty last night. The guy was fried. I smelled the burning flesh as soon as I went into the basement. He was changing fuses."

"How did that electrocute him?" asked Tony.

"There was a puddle of water in front of the fuse box. They had one of those old-fashioned washing machines. You know the type with the wringer on top? Well, the drain in that thing was a rubber hose with a metal hook-shaped end. You're supposed to hook that into a wash tub, but this one was lying on the basement floor. There's always water left in the hose and with the end lying on the floor, it drained out. The fuse box was right next to the wash tub and a puddle formed in front of the fuse box. When he touched the fuse, Zappo!"

"Was he alone in the house?"

"No, his wife was there. She said the power went out and he went down to change fuses."

"Did she say anything about the hose being on the floor?"

"Yeah, she said she didn't leave it that way. She always hooks it into the wash tub. I guess it's just a freak accident."

* * *

Forty-five minutes later, Tony knocked on the door of the Jenkins home.

"Mrs. Jenkins?" Tony said to the woman who opened the door. Her eyes were red-rimmed but she was composed.

"Yes, I'm Mrs. Jenkins. Can I help you?"

"I'm, Tony Donohoo, New Jersey State Detective. I am sorry to bother you at a time like this, but I think this is important. I met your husband the other day and he was to call me back. Can you tell me if he was one of the jurors in the Cassetti murder trial back in 1947?" Mrs. Jenkins studied his badge and ID card for a few moments.

"Please come in, Detective. Yes, he was on that trial.

Why?" She led the way into a small, inexpensively furnished living room. Tony sat at Mrs. Jenkins hand motion.

"Do you know who any of the other jurors were?"

"No. I don't. He didn't like to talk about it. Especially after they found out Cassetti wasn't the murderer. One thing he said at the time was that Cassetti was guilty as hell."

"What about when he found out somebody else did it?"

"He didn't talk about it."

"Mrs. Jenkins—"

"Call me Gertrude."

"All right, Gertrude. Charlie is at least the third of those jurors to die in what appears to be accidents just in the last few months. There may be more, but so far I've identified only four of the jurors. I think some self-appointed avenger is making it his business to mete out the death penalty in some deranged retribution. I told Charlie this on Tuesday."

"He said not a word about this to me. Do you think I'm safe?" Mrs. Jenkins face had taken on an expression of total fear.

"I can't answer that. Everything I've learned so far indicates the former jurors to be the targets, but at this stage of the investigation, I know very little. Here's my card. If anything else comes to you, give me a call. By the way, is that your Pontiac in the driveway?"

"Yes, it is."

"Did Charlie use that car?"

"Very rarely. He had the use of dealership cars."

"Can you give me a recent picture of Charlie? It will help people I interview who won't know him by his name."

Gertrude nodded and left the room, returning in a minute with a photograph.

"If you wouldn't mind, just write your address and phone number in my notebook," Tony said.

Gertrude nodded compliance.

"Thank you. I'll have copies made of the photo and return the original shortly. My last request is to take a look at your basement."

Tony descended into the dank and dirty, musty basement. One bare bulb hung from a frayed black electric wire, casting eerie shadows. A workbench with a smattering of tools stood by the rear wall. The stained laundry sink was mounted alongside an old washing machine; its drain hose hooked over the sink. And then the fuse box. A door with a skeleton key lock led to concrete steps shielded from the weather by wooden hurricane doors in disrepair. The door lock was rusty and did not appear to be currently used.

"The basement doesn't look like it could be locked," said Tony when he returned to the first floor.

"No, that old lock hasn't worked in years. We have a sliding bolt on the inside of the basement door in the kitchen. I'd been after Charlie to seal up the basement steps to the back yard, but he never got around to it - like a lot of other things."

"I'll leave you now, Gertrude. Again, you have my sympathy. Please call if anything comes to mind."

Tony made note of the license plate number on the Pontiac in the driveway. While at the Buick dealer, he had recorded the dealer's license plate number, DBE 16. The

"D" in DBE stood for dealer. Those plates could be interchanged on any vehicle. The dealership had dozens of them with the only differentiation being small consecutive numbers following the numerals 16. The dealer was only required to keep a log book on which plate was placed on which car. Their policy was to assign a particular plate number to a salesman and as he changed demo cars, the plate was also changed. Charlie's plate number had been DBE 16-11.

* * *

"Hey, Andy Panda, I'll take a bottle of Schlitz," Tony said on his second visit to O'Neill's Bar and Grill.

"Coming right up," Andy said, but without the smile he wore on Tony's first visit to O'Neill's. "Andy, I found your car salesman guy from the jury. I talked to him on Tuesday. Last night he was electrocuted in his basement. It's in the afternoon paper."

Andy stood transfixed. Finally, he spoke. "What do you think it means?"

"Three former jurors die in what appear to be accidents within a few months. The odds against three coincidences just went through the roof. If I were you, I'd get the hell out of town for a while. Then give me a telephone call collect and tell me how you can be reached. You could be next. And I still don't know if there weren't others because only four of the jurors are known to me."

"I can't just leave. I've got a job. My wife has a job."

"Yeah, well, you'll be out of a job when your turn comes. Charlie Jenkins—that was the car salesman—has sold his last car. He didn't take me seriously and he's in the morgue. I've got my camera. I want to get a shot of you."

"What for?"

"I'm investigating. In talking to other jurors, when and if I find them, I show the pictures just like I did with you when I showed you Marcy Cavanagh's photo. Also, write down your address, home number and the number here."

Andy took the pen and wrote in Tony's notebook."Okay, but I don't see—"

"Just smile for the god damned camera, Andy. And get the hell out of town."

NINE

Tony arrived at the office to find Mindy at work on the blackboard. On one side she had written "Interviews to be done." On the other side she had written "Suspects."

Under "Interviews:"
    Harry Cassetti, Jr.
    Stephen Cassetti
    Cassetti neighbors in 1947
    Mrs. Beatrice Jackson
    Jackson's neighbors
    Cavanagh's Maywood neighbors
    Cavanagh's Sunrise Lake neighbors
    Jenkins' neighbors

Under "Suspects:"
    Andy Panda
    Jurors number 5 through 12
    Louis Notella
    Robert Anton Haines
    Judge Malcolm Willcox
    Gertrude Jenkins
    Beatrice Jackson
    Brendan Cavanagh

Spouses of Andy Panda and Jurors number 5 through 12
Harry Cassetti Jr.
Stephen Cassetti
Ezekiel Fussbucket (Tony's name for a person yet to be known)

At the bottom of the blackboard, Mindy had listed three questions.

1. How does the killer know the names of the jurors?
2. Is the killer a deranged avenger?
3. Is this a "fishnet" killer?

The fishnet guy catches a bunch of fish in a net, but only wants one to eat. The fishnet killer wipes out a bunch of people with something in common, yet only one is the real target, and the others disguise the killer's motive.

"Good job, Mindy," said Tony. "Especially question number one. We're breaking our asses trying to get the jurors' names, while whoever is doing the killings obviously knows who they are. How does he know?"

"Haines and Notella would know. Judges Willcox and Huber would know." Mindy said.

TEN

Friday, October 16, 1953, 9:05 A.M. - Chambers of Assignment Judge Endicott Huber

"The judge will see you now, Miss," said the clerk.

Mindy rose and entered.

"Good morning, Judge. My name is Mindy McCall and I'm a private investigator. My agency has been retained to look into the death of Marcy Cavanagh, who served as a juror in the Cassetti trial of 1947."

"Take a seat, Miss. I have only a few minutes, so, please be brief. I recall that case, though I didn't preside. Judge Willcox, if memory serves."

"Yes, your honor. Three of those former jurors have been killed in the last few months in what appear to be accidents but could easily be murder. The last one, Charles Jenkins, occurred this week.

My agency has identified only four of those jurors and three are dead. We 're hoping that you will give the order to open the file and give us the names of the remaining eight jurors."

"Why would I do that?"

"First and foremost, to allow us to warn them that some deranged person seems to be knocking off the Cassetti jurors. Secondly, to find the murderer."

"You say these deaths were ruled as accidents?" asked the judge.

"Yes, Your Honor."

"Well, perhaps that's exactly what they were."

"But three in a matter of months? Don't you think that's beyond coincidence?"

"I'm not sure of the mathematical probabilities, but there have been stranger coincidences."

"Perhaps those weren't really coincidences either, Judge. At what point between three and twelve would you acknowledge a pattern?"

"You're not being impertinent, are you, young lady?"

"Maybe just a touch, Judge. But it is a legitimate question."

"I don't choose to quantify it," said the judge.

"And you won't, as of now, release those names?"

"I will not."

"Could you have your clerk check to find out if other jurors have died? Lives could be at stake."

"You will now excuse me, Miss McCall. The clerk will see you out."

* * *

Tony parked in front of a small, neatly painted two-story house. White pebbles in a rock garden patch spelled out

"Jackson." A single car garage in matching white with blue trim stood at the left-rear corner of the lot. Similar houses abutted on both sides. Mature landscaping and shrubbery growth provided privacy, although the lot was not big.

In answer to Tony's ringing the doorbell, a comely woman in her late thirties came to the door. She wore a neat white uniform with shoes to match and a black pinafore.

After introducing himself, Tony asked: "Are you Mrs. Beatrice Jackson?"

"Yes, I am. Is something wrong?" .

"I'm investigating several curious deaths of late, including your husband's. I have a few questions for you. Is this a good time?"

She held the door wide and motioned Tony to enter. "I have to leave for work in twenty minutes. I've had to take a job since Norman died. I'm working as a waitress at Petrullo's Everglades. What do you want to know?"

"First, I want to confirm something. My information is that your husband served as a juror in the Cassetti trial in 1947. Is that true?"

"Yes, he did. How did you know that?"

"At least three of those jurors have died in the last five months. Your husband, a Maywood woman, and just two days ago, an Englewood man. All Cassetti jurors. Did you have any suspicions that Norman's death might not have been an accident?"

"No, I didn't. Of course, this is the first I've heard of these other deaths."

"I know that all twelve jurors voted to convict Harry Cassetti. How strongly did Norman feel about that?"

"Well, they were sequestered so I didn't speak to Norman about anything until the trial was over. What little he said about it was that he was convinced that Cassetti was guilty."

"What about when he found out that somebody else actually did the crime?"

"I think he kind of blamed the lawyers...and the judge."

"At this time, the court will not release the names of the jurors. My immediate objective is to identify them. First, to alert them to danger and second, to find the killer who appears to be intent on meting out revenge. Can you help me identify any of the other jurors?"

"No, I never met any of them. I don't think Norman even knew their names, and if he did, it's been years."

"Do you have any children?"

"No, no children," she said wistfully.

"Were you at home when Norman was killed?"

"No, I was shopping. I came home and made lunch. I called Norman to come in to eat. He was out in the garage working on his car. When he didn't answer, I went out...." she broke off and started to sob.

"I am sorry to bring this up. Did you notice anyone loitering in the neighborhood? Any strange cars parked nearby? It could have been several days before."

"No, I can't say that I did."

"I presume you held a wake?"

"Yes, a wake and then a funeral."

"I would like to borrow the sign-in book from the funeral

home. Do you have it?'

"Yes, I have it. I'll get it for you, but what do you think you'll find?"

"I don't know. Maybe nothing. I'll make sure to return it. Oh, by the way, take my notebook and write your address and phone number where I can reach you."

Mrs. Jackson nodded agreement."The car in the driveway—is that the one you've generally used?"

"Yes, why?"

"Just routine. What about the one Norman used?"

"It's in the garage. I'm going to sell it."

"Would you mind if I took a look at it."

"Sure, go ahead. I don't know what that will tell you."

"It's just routine. By the way," said Tony, shifting gears, "I notice that photograph of you with, I'm guessing, Norman. Could I borrow that photo? I'll copy it and return the original in a few days."

"I suppose so - but why would you need it?"

"The other jurors probably never knew or have forgotten the names of their fellow jurors, but might recognize him from a photo. It helps in the investigation. Again, just routine."

* * *

Back at the office, Tony put in a call to Brendan Cavanagh.

"Brendan, Tony Donohoo here. I wanted to touch base with you. First, we have identified two more of the jurors. I met with them. One guy I met on Tuesday was electrocuted in his basement Wednesday night."

"I read that in the paper yesterday. That guy was one of the jurors?"

"Yeah, I tried to warn him but the stupid bastard outsmarted me and now he's dead."

"So how do you feel now, with three of them dead?"

"I think you're right. We've interviewed both lawyers and the judge, Mindy McCall, an operative of mine, is going to try to interview the assignment judge today. He's the one that decides whether the file can be opened up to reveal the names of the other jurors. And I've got an ad running in the paper that I hope will yield results."

"Well, you have made progress. What's next?"

"Tomorrow morning, I'm going up to Sunrise Lake to look around. Talk to the neighbors, if any are around, maybe a few of the merchants."

"Do you have any reason to get into my cabin?"

"It couldn't hurt. You never know."

"All right, I'll tell you where we hide the key," said Cavanagh.

"Don't tell me. It's hanging on a nail in the outdoor shower."

"How did you know that?"

"Did I forget to tell you I'm a detective?"

Cavanagh laughed out loud. "I guess that's where everybody hides the key to a summer house. Hey, bring it back with you. Next time I'm up there, I'll find a better hiding place."

"Oh, one last thing, Brendan. I presume you held a wake and a funeral?"

"Yeah, sure I did."

"The funeral parlor would have given you the sign-in book."

"Yeah, I got it."

"Well, get it to me, will you?"

"You think the killer would have gone to the wake? And then signed in?"

"We can safely conclude the killer is bad. We haven't gotten to smart yet."

"I'll drop it off," said Brendan.

* * *

"So how did your meeting with Judge Huber go?" asked Tony.

"He's a pompous, close-minded, self-centered asshole and a nasty old bastard sonofabitch," said Mindy, venting.

"So, you don't like him?" said Tony, grinning ear-to-ear.

"When I asked him how many dead people it would take for him to unseal the records, he said, and I quote, 'I don't choose to quantify it.' What kind of a judge could he be?"

"I agree with you. He shouldn't be on the bench. Anybody who deliberately pisses off a good-looking redhead is using poor judgment and that says it all."

ELEVEN

By 6:45, Tony and Mindy were ordering egg drop soup and chicken chow mein at Hing's China Inn in Englewood Cliffs.

"What do you think I should do tomorrow? " asked Mindy.

"How about hitting the neighbors around Cavanagh's house in Maywood? After that you might see what you can learn of the whereabouts of the Cassetti boys. They'd be well into their twenties by now."

"What are you going to do?"

The Chinese waiter served the egg drop soup. Mindy nodded and smiled at him. He smiled back.

"I'm going up to Sunrise Lake and see if anybody saw anything. I'm also hoping that by tomorrow we'll get a response or two from the ad asking former jurors to come forth," Tony said.

"It's October. Do you think there'll be anyone at the lake?

"What are you saying? Wait until next June? Cavanagh said they used their cabin on weekends until Thanksgiving. Maybe some of the neighbors do the same," Tony said.

"Okay, now comes the big question. What movie do you want to see? *Monkey Business* with Cary Grant and Ginger Rogers is at the Plaza Theater or *Big Jim McClain* with John Wayne at the Fox Theater."

"I'll go for *Monkey Business,*" said Tony.

"We saw the coming attractions for that last week. You just want to see that new girl, Marilyn Monroe. You have a thing for her. I can tell."

"She's not bad, but I wouldn't call it a thing. It's just a movie. Charles Coburn is in it, too. I've always been a big fan of Charles Coburn."

"Kiss me before you lie to me. I like to get kissed before I get screwed." Mindy said

After the movie, they went to Tony's apartment. Tony, in anticipation of Mindy staying over, had that morning put fresh sheets on the bed and cleaned the bathroom. By midnight, all was right with the world. A mental picture of Marilyn Monroe flitted through his mind once or twice, but he kept that from the curvy redhead in his bed.

* * *

Saturday, October 18, 1953, 8:00 A.M.

Tony awoke to sounds of Mindy in the kitchen. He brushed his teeth and stumbled out to meet the day. Tony's apartment was over the real estate office and next to the Yellow Front Saloon. He had a living room, two bedrooms (the smaller of which had been converted into a dark room), and a kitchen large enough to house a dining room set for eight, an easy chair and a TV set. Curio cabinets hung in several locations holding Tony's pewter collection. One cabinet had tiny statues of presidents and founding fathers, another of mythical animals: unicorns, satyrs and the like. Another shelf contained lions, bears and a single giraffe. Cathedrals and famous landmark structures were in a different case and lastly the transportation collection of cars, trucks, trains and airplanes. Mindy referred to the collection as "Tony's feminine side."

"I hate your god damned kitchen, you know that? I hate yellow. You had your sister-in-law decorate and apparently, she loves yellow. So your pots and pans, dishes and coffee pot are all yellow. The knives and forks have yellow handles. The clock is yellow." Nevertheless, Mindy had a few rashers of bacon frying in the yellow frying pan. She poured him a yellow cup of coffee. Wearing no makeup, her freckles were showing. Tony's terry cloth bathrobe came almost to her ankles. Giving an extra wiggle, she parked herself on Tony's lap, put her arms around his neck and kissed him on the lips.

"I'll forgo breakfast for another go-round," he said, while lighting up his first Lucky of the day.

"No can do, big boy. We have work to do."

"I'll throw in re-painting the kitchen - and buying all new utensils. What color would you like?"

"Cut the crap, Tony. You're going up to Sunrise Lake. Any more suggestions on what I should do?"

"I've been thinking that before you do anything else, you should canvas the neighbors around Charlie Jenkins' house.

If they saw anything suspicious that night, it's better to get them while it might be fresh in their minds. Someone must have been there at the house Wednesday night, but he or she also must have checked the place out at some earlier time. Otherwise the killer wouldn't know that the clothes washer was next to the fuse box."

"Sounds good. I have a photo shoot scheduled for four o'clock so I'm free up till then." Spatula in hand, she placed two eggs sunny-side-up, bacon and buttered toast in front of Tony, and a similar plate for herself.

* * *

By 9:15, Tony and Mindy were underway. He dropped her at her apartment, where her car was parked, and got started on the ninety-mile trip north into New York State. Tony was in sport coat and fedora, but left his .38 snub-nose at home. His commission as a New Jersey State Detective wouldn't be suitable documentation to carry a concealed weapon in New York.

Tony rolled into the Village of Sunrise Lake at 11:45. An old lunch wagon, now up on blocks, carried a hand-painted sign reading "Bobbi Jo's Beanery." Tony figured he would grab an early lunch and see what Bobbi Jo knew of the drowning. One old guy, surely a townie, sat nursing a cup of coffee at the counter. The depth of the place was only about ten feet, which left no room for tables. At the end of the place was a window for pickup orders. Tony hopped on a stool, then spun it around to take in the panorama of the lake.

"I'll take the tuna fish salad sandwich on rye with a side of cole slaw," Tony said after checking out the menu card. "And a cup of coffee—black. You Bobbi Jo?"

"That's me."

Bobbi Jo could have been around to welcome the dough boys home from France. Her voice had a two-pack-a-day rasp and a lit Camel dangled from her lips. She placed the coffee in front of him and got to work on the sandwich. When the sandwich was placed before him, Tony said "Been in business long?"

"Since 1921. Didn't you see the sign outside?"

"Yeah, I saw it, but I figured you're not old enough to have started the place."

"Before you try to sweet talk me again, that'll be 95 cents."

Tony threw two bucks on the counter and said "keep the change."

"You're leaving me a tip that's larger than the bill. Whatdya want?"

"Maybe just a little information." Tony presented his shield and introduced himself. "I'm up from Jersey to look into the drowning death of a woman named Marcy Cavanagh in July. Can you tell me anything about it?"

"Not much. Just what I heard around," said Bobbi Jo.

"Did you know her?"

"She was in here with her kids a few times. Nice lady. Pretty. What's to find out, anyway? She drowned. Wasn't the first time it's happened and won't be the last.."

"I'm investigating. It was probably just an accident. I hope it was. Did you notice anybody hanging around, any strange cars?"

"In July, we're up to our eyeballs with city folk. Who would notice one more? There's five, maybe six hundred cabins around the lake. Some on the water and some on the up side of Sunrise Circle. In summer the population swells to tenfold what it is now. After Labor Day, we're left with a couple of hundred locals. Hey Gus?"

"What?" said the man at the counter.

"This is a Jersey cop. He wants to know if we saw anything the day that woman drowned."

"I didn't see nothing."

Tony didn't bother to contradict being called a cop. He swung around again on his stool and looked out across the lake. On the other side, about 400 yards away, he could see a turned over white lifeguard stand on a small sandy beach. "Is that where she drowned?" he said, pointing.

"Yeah, that's the spot," answered Bobbi Jo. "In summer, they anchor a raft off the shore. You can see it on the beach. It's light blue. See it? They found her underneath the raft."

"Was the lifeguard on duty?"

"I think she swam early in the morning before the lifeguard came on."

"Well, thanks, you've been helpful," said Tony, taking the last bite of his sandwich and swilling down the rest of his coffee. "Maybe I'll check out the general store and the barber shop."

"Barber shop's only open Monday and Tuesday during

the off season. Guido works at a big barber shop over in Cooperstown the rest of the week," said Gus. "If I were you, I'd talk to Smitty down in the boat yard. If he ain't out painting rowboats, he's in his shack. He's the only one who gets in early enough to have seen anything. That woman drowned real early in the morning. I'd talk to Smitty."

Tony stopped at the general store which also maintained the post office franchise. About 100 boxes were accessible to customers, each with a combination wheel. "Is there any mail delivery here?" Tony asked of the only visible employee, a young woman in blue jeans.

"This is as far as it comes. The boxes out here are for the locals. We have slots in the back for the summer people."

Tony asked if she knew Marcy Cavanagh.

"I know that's the lady that drowned this summer. I guess she was in here but I don't know which one she was. They don't pick up mail here."

He strolled across the street and down a short way to "Smitty's Boatyard." As Gus had indicated, a man was stenciling the name of the enterprise in white paint on freshly painted rowboats in blue, orange, red, green, purple and yellow.

"You Smitty?"

"That's me. Who're you?"

"Tony Donohoo, New Jersey State Detective." He flashed his shield and ID.

"What brings you up here?"

"I'm checking on the drowning of a woman named Marcy Cavanagh, back in May. I know it's hard to remember after five months, but do you have any recollection of that day?"

"Ain't hard at all."

"You do remember? What do you remember?"

"I remember seeing a woman swimming out toward the other side of the lake. Early. About six thirty in the morning. She wore a rubber bathing cap. Orange."

"Where did she enter the water?"

"Can't say for sure. I only saw her when she was maybe a hundred yards out."

"You're sure it was the same day?"

"I'm sure," said Smitty.

"How can you be sure?"

"Because when I heard about the drowning later that morning, I figured the lady I saw with the orange cap was the one who drowned."

"So the closest you were to the swimmer was at least several hundred feet?"

"Right."

"How do you know it was a woman?"

"I ain't never seen no man wear one of them bathing caps, have you?"

"Did you see if she got to the other side of the lake?"

"Didn't notice. Probably didn't look again," said Smitty.

Tony drove around the lake and found the Cavanagh cabin. It was on a lot about sixty feet wide on a slight incline down to the water's edge. A narrow wooden dock extended about twenty feet into the lake. Two canoes had been dragged out of the water and turned over. Tony found a fallen branch and walked out to the end of the dock to test the depth of the water It was about six feet deep at that point.

Like many of its fellows, the Cavanagh house was an authentic log cabin. Tony removed the key from its nail in the outdoor shower and went in. The building was about 25 by 30 feet. The first floor contained a living-dining room with a fireplace, a small kitchen and a bedroom. The furniture was old but serviceable. There were two other sleeping areas in a loft open to the first floor and accessed by a steep log staircase. The stairs and the inside of the perimeter walls were black logs shiny with preservative stain. The only significant modernization to the old cabin was a shed-like attachment off the kitchen which housed a toilet and wash sink. The appliances were dated but not original. The kitchen was equipped with the usual tools, pots and pans, flatware and utensils. A smattering of canned goods and non-perishable staples occupied the pantry shelves. The refrigerator door was propped open. No power was on.

As Tony exited the front door, a voice called out: "Can we help you?" which he took to mean, "What are you doing here and what do you want?" Two men, one fifty-ish and one in his twenties—clearly father and son—stood near Tony's parked car, their legs parted in territorial protectiveness. A woman, hovered on the porch next door with alarm etched into her face.

"New Jersey State Detective Donohoo," answered Tony flashing his tin. "I'm investigating the death of Marcy Cavanagh. Brendan Cavanagh knows I'm here. I'll tell him he's lucky to have neighbors keeping an eye on things. What's your name?"

"My name's Al Zipoli. My son, Joe. This is our cabin here." He motioned to the one next door. "Yeah, we look out for one another," said the elder. "But I don't get the investigation. She just drowned. What's to investigate?"

"Yeah, she drowned but what was the cause? Did somebody hold her head under water? Or was it an accident? That's what I'm looking into. Were you up here when it happened?"

"I was. My son wasn't."

"Did you see anyone hanging around a day or two before?"

"No, can't say I did."

"Any strange cars?"

"Nothing comes to mind."

"What about the missus?"

The woman, who had not spoken, just shook her head.

"I'm told Mrs. Cavanagh was swimming alone. Was that unusual?"

"No, she did that all the time," said the son.

"Did she walk down to that little beach?"

"No, she'd dive right off their dock."

"Here's my card. Please call me if you think of anything? Oh, one more thing. Did Marcy Cavanagh ever wear an orange rubber bathing cap?"

Father and son looked at each other and both shook their heads. "Marcy didn't wear bathing caps at all," said Mrs. Zipoli from her porch.

"Did you ever notice anyone else wearing an orange one?" All three shook their heads.

After taking note of the Jersey license plates on the two cars in Zipoli's front yard, Tony got on the road, having observed no cars parked by any of the other cabins nearby.

* * *

After Tony dropped her off at 9:15 A.M., Mindy went up to her apartment and applied her makeup. She picked out a skirt and jacket of navy blue and heels to match. She hopped into her '51 Kelly green Ford convertible and drove over to Hamilton Avenue in Englewood to check out the Jenkins's neighbors. Having checked out the abutting houses and the ones across the street with no results, she drove around the block to interview those that backed up to the Jenkins house. Still no luck. No one she spoke to had seen any strangers hanging around.

Next stop was the former Cassetti neighborhood. The Cassetti house itself, on Bennett Road in Teaneck, was now owned and occupied by someone else. After knocking on four or five doors, Mindy found the neighborhood gossip monger. The lady, a Mrs. Greco, seemed proud of her knowledge of Bennett Road and was eager to share. Her world was Bennett Road and no visitor, no delivery, nothing escaped her attention.

"The oldest boy, Harry Jr." said Mrs. Greco, "joined the army right after his mother was killed. He's making a career of it. Right now he's in Korea."

"So, you don't think he's been around New Jersey in the last few months?"

"No. He shipped out last winter. He has a close friend who lived up the street. Gerard Cummings. Number seventeen. He would know Harry's whereabouts."

"What about the younger brother? Steven?" asked Mindy.

"Before the father's trial, he went to live in Bridgeport, Connecticut, with his aunt and uncle. Steven took their name: Kilmurray. If you talk to Gerard, he'll know the address."

"When was the last time you saw Steven?"

"Not since he left."

At 17 Bennett Road, Mindy spoke to Gerard Cummings' father. Gerard, he said, was working at the hardware store on Cedar Lane. Mindy found the store and asked for Gerard. She was directed out to the rear of the store where he was taking a smoke break.

"Yeah, I saw Harry last January," Gerard said in answer to Mindy's query. "He was on leave before shipping out to Korea. I'm guessing with the cease fire, he'll be back soon, but he may not come here but to his new post. He's regular army, a thirty-year man."

"Do you write to him?"

"Yeah, once in a while."

"So you have his address?"

"Yeah. Not with me. Gimme a card or something. I'll get it to you."

"What do you know about his brother, Steven?" Mindy

asked, as she slipped him her card.

"Steve took a different name - his aunt's married name. Kilmurray. He lives in Bridgeport with his aunt and uncle. Last I heard, he was a bartender."

"When did you see him last?

"Gotta be a year, maybe more."

"He looked you up when he came back to visit?" asked Mindy.

"No, the other way around. I was passing through Bridgeport and I called him. We went out and had a pizza and a few beers. Funny, up there they spell it a-p-i-z-z-a, and they say it *ah - petes.*"

"Can you get me his address, too?"

"Sure thing. I'll call your office with both of them."

"How did he and Harry feel about the father finally being exonerated?"

"They weren't broken up over it. They both hated their father and how he treated their mother. He beat the mother up routinely and smacked the two brothers around all the time growing up. Turns out he didn't kill her, but he was an out-and-out prick nevertheless. Pardon my French."

"So, do you think either one of them might hold a grudge about his being wrongly convicted and executed?"

"I don't see how they could. They thought he was guilty."

TWELVE

Tony arrived back at his office about four o'clock. Alice, the receptionist Tony shared with the real estate agency, was gone for the day. She had left two telephone messages on his desk:

> *Sat 10/17 1 PM*
> *Mrs Bankowski called*
> *about the ad in the*
> *Record. LO 8 1502*
> *Alice*
>
> *Sat 10/17 2:15 PM*
> *A man called about*
> *the ad in the Record*
> *Refused to leave a*
> *name or number.*
> *Said he'd call back.*
> *Alice*

Tony dialed Mrs. Bankowski's number. She picked up on the second ring.

"Mrs. Bankowski, this is Tony Donohoo. You called earlier?"

"Yes, I did. I want to know what you meant in that ad you ran."

"I thought the ad was pretty straight forward. I believe those former jurors may be in danger."

"But why do you think that?"

"Perhaps it would be better if I met with you and we discussed this," said Tony.

"You're a private detective, right?"

"Yes."

"Well, if w—uh - the former jurors are in danger, why aren't the police looking into this?"

"I'll explain all that—and everything else—when we meet. You can come to my office or I can go to you, or if you want to meet in some public place, just name it."

"Well, all right. Today?"

"Yeah, today's okay."

"How about the Star Diner in Englewood in thirty minutes?"

"I know the place and I'll see you there," said Tony. "How will I know you?"

"I'll wear a green coat."

* * *

Tony waited in a booth with a cup of coffee. A blue '52 Plymouth pulled in and a large woman wearing a kerchief and a green coat got out. Tony scribbled down the license plate number. He rose when she entered the diner and waved her over. Mrs. Bankowski was a pleasant-looking woman with a bland expression in her late forties. She wore a somewhat hesitant smile, and took the seat Tony offered.

"Would you like something? Coffee? A Danish?"

"Just a cup of tea, thank you." She held her purse tightly with one hand.

Tony spread the four photos he had on the table. "These are four of the twelve people who served on the Cassetti trial back in 1947. These three," pushing aside Andy Panda's picture, "have died in questionable accidents in the last five months. This one, Charlie Jenkins, just a couple of days ago. The court records are sealed. These are the only four jurors I know about. I want to find the other eight."

" I remember these people now that I see their faces. I couldn't have told you their names. You said 'questionable accidents.' What's a questionable—I don't know what you mean. What do you mean?"

"Marcy Cavanagh drowned while swimming alone at an upstate lake. Norman Jackson was crushed to death by his car while he was underneath. The jack slipped. Charlie Jenkins was electrocuted while trying to change a fuse in the dark, unaware that he was standing in a puddle of water from the washing machine."

"You're saying they weren't accidents. How do you know - I mean they might have been accidents. How do you know they weren't?" asked Mrs. Bankowski.

"I don't *know*, know. But the odds of three out of the twelve people who served on the jury dying by accidents in a few months are going through the roof."

"Are you trying to get me to pay you money—to hire you?"

"No, I have a client."

"But why don't the police - I mean, why aren't the police doing this? Wouldn't they be working on this if it were a real threat?"

"Three people died in three different districts. One was even out of state. In each case, the local authorities ruled it an accident. None of the three districts knew of the other deaths. I've answered your questions. Now you tell me. You were one of the jurors, weren't you?"

"Yes. I feel terrible about it. I've had nightmares since I found out Cassetti wasn't guilty.

He was a human being and we took his life."

"You didn't take his life. Judge Willcox took his life. He could have overruled the jury's verdict or he could have accepted it and sentenced Cassetti to twenty years or life. If he had, Cassetti would be walking around now. He's not because of the judge's sentence. End of story. How did you feel about the trial. Did you think Cassetti was guilty or not?"

"I didn't know. Some people were so sure. I just - I mean, how can you know? I didn't know. A lot of the others seemed to know."

"Now," Tony continued, "you're the fifth juror. Can you help me identify the other seven?'

"What will you do when you know who they are? Or any one of them?"

THE CASE OF THE DEAD JURORS • 81

"Just what I'm doing with you. First, warn them they may be in danger. Second, find out who the killer is."

"So, you think I'm in danger?"

"Of course, I think you're in danger. Don't you?"

"I just find it hard to accept."

"What's your first name?"

"My name is Malina. You can call me that."

"Well, Malina, do you have a family?"

"I'm married, three grown children. Two grandchildren."

"Do your children live around here?"

"Two of them do. My daughter lives in Moscow, Pennsylvania, with her husband and little boy."

"I urge you to go and stay with her until we get to the bottom of this. She has a married name?" Malina nodded.

"Good, it'll be difficult to trace. You should be safe there, but stay alert. Avoid being alone. Now you seemed a little reluctant to help me find the other jurors. What about that?"

"Well, there's only one I can name. We became friends after serving together on the jury. We met for lunch a couple of times a year. Her name was Kathleen Geiger, but it won't do you any good."

"Why not?"

"Because she's dead."

"She's dead? She's dead? That's what I'm talking about, for God's sake. Tell me about it."

"But her death can't have anything to do with this."

"No? Why not?"

"She didn't die in an accident. She committed suicide."

"When? Where? How?"

"In her house in Paramus. In June. She hung herself."

"I'm gonna take your picture. Then you go home, pack a bag, and go to your daughter's house. Your life is in danger." Tony produced his notebook and passed it over to her. "Put your daughter's name, address and phone number down, just in case I have to reach you., and your address and number here in Englewood. Tell your husband if he wants to talk to me, he can call me or come to my office."

THIRTEEN

I will keep my promise true
Till I waltz again with you.

The Jukebox sounded the haunting voice of Theresa Brewer, as Tony and Mindy found a table. Tony often said the Park View Tavern in Englewood had the best thin-crust pizza in New Jersey. Tony gave the order including a Schlitz for himself and a Pabst's Blue Ribbon for Mindy.

Tony shared his experiences of the day ending with the suicide of Kathleen Geiger. "This woman, Malina Bankowski, can hardly get a complete thought out. Very unsure of herself. She interrupts her own sentences, stammers a lot. I can't picture her having to commit herself on a capital offense."

"Well, that's four. Maybe I'll take another shot at Judge Huber."

"Better yet," said Tony, "We'll send him a letter and copy Judge Willcox and Louis Notella. He won't want to refuse when there's a record of the request."

"It looks like Harry Cassetti Jr. is out of it. He's been in Korea since January. The other boy, Stephen, lives in Connecticut with his aunt." She related how they both hated the father and believed the jury got it right. "So it would be unlikely they would hold some grudge."

"We'll have to verify that Harry Jr. has been in Korea all year. And the fact that the younger brother changed his name supports the story that he's no fan of his late father, but you better talk to him anyway," said Tony.

"Don't get any of that stuff on my side of the pizza," Mindy cautioned when Tony began to sprinkle crushed red pepper on the pie. "What are you going to do tomorrow?"

"I'll go check out the suicide of Kathleen Geiger in Paramus. If you would, the license plates we've collected on this case need to be posted and cross referenced."

"Yeah, okay. But I don't think the license plate file is going to be of much help on this one."

"You never know. There might be a surprise in there. Anyway, there's always the chance that the killer will return to the scene of the crime, so to speak. He might not go to the Jenkins house, but he might just show up at the guy's wake, just to feel superior."

* * *

At a few minutes past eight o'clock, Tony and Mindy parked across the street from the Timothy P. Kelly Home for Funerals in Dumont. Gertrude Jenkins had ordered a one night wake. The lot was nearly full when Tony and Mindy got out of the car and began to take down all the plate numbers. There were many with the plate numbered DDE 16, followed by the tiny sequential number, Charlie's co-workers from the dealership. Three men came out and stood on the portico of the building smoking. They took notice of Mindy, who was closer, going car to car and writing on a yellow pad. They strolled over to her.

"What do you think you're doing, girlie?" asked one.

"She's taking down license plate numbers," called out Tony, approaching the group. "So am I."

"Why you doing that?" asked the man, with anger rising.

"Because we want to know who's at the wake," answered Mindy, with implication that it was a stupid question.

"Yeah," said a second man, "maybe you ought to shove off. Now."

"And maybe you three ought to shove off. Now," said Tony producing his shield.

"Don't you have no respect for the dead?" asked the third man.

"Do you want to be charged with impeding an investigation?" The three of them grumbled and walked back to the building..

By ten o'clock, Tony and Mindy were sitting at the bar in the Yellow Front Saloon, kibitzing with some of the regulars. Tony's brother, Frankie, joined them for a drink.

"*Citizen Kane* is on the Late Show," Frankie said. "I know that's a favorite of yours."

"We can't miss that," Tony said.

At eleven o'clock he whispered in Mindy's ear "Let's drink up."

The two of them climbed the stairs to Tony's apartment

and settled to cuddle on the sofa. At eleven-fifteen came the sounds of LeRoy Anderson's *Syncopated Clock,* followed by the movie.

"I saw this when I was in junior high," said Mindy. "Charles Foster Kane was the character's name. Wasn't there some mystery over his last words? 'Rosebud'?"

"Yeah. It was written on his sled when he was a kid. But did you ever hear why they used it in the movie?"

Mindy shook her head.

"It's based on the life of William Randolph Hearst and his mistress, Marion Davies, the actress. Apparently, Orson Welles, who played Kane but also directed and co-wrote the screenplay, got wind of a story that Hearst had a pet name for Marion's pleasure patch and wanted to rub it in, just to piss off Hearst a little more."

"Well, what was the pet name?" Mindy asked.

"Rosebud."

FOURTEEN

Sunday, October 18, 1953, 9:45 A.M.

Paramus Police Headquarters was all but deserted on Sunday morning. There was just one cop in the building working the desk and dispatching calls.

"Tony Donohoo," he said flashing his shield.

"What's your problem?"

"I'm looking into the death of a local woman back in June. Her name was Kathleen Geiger. Can you tell me whose case it was?"

"Hold on, let me check the file." After being interrupted by two incoming calls, both of which required the cop to radio cars on patrol, he returned with the file. "Lieutenant Charlie Kennis."

"Any chance I could take a look at the file?"

"Sure, there's an excellent chance, provided Kennis gives the okay, but he ain't here."

"Can you call him?"

"Let me see if I got this straight. You want me to call Kennis on a Sunday morning to tell him that a private dick wants to look over his file. Is that about it?"

"Yeah, that's about it," Tony answered.

"Take a walk, pal."

"Does he live in town?"

"You're the private dick. Figure it out."

"The pleasure was all mine, officer."

Tony's next stop was the Route 17 Diner. He got a cup of coffee and checked out the phone book in the public booth. Charles Kennis was listed living in Paramus. Tony dialed the number.

"Hello."

"Have I got Lieutenant Kennis?"

"Who's this?"

"Sorry, this is Tony Donohoo. I'm a private detective from Hackensack. I'm looking into the death of Kathleen Geiger back in June. The officer on duty said you were in charge of that case."

"Who you working for?"

"It's kind of a detailed story, but it's not the family of the deceased. Any chance I could meet with you and I'll explain?"

"I'm going to the eleven o'clock mass. If you want, I'll meet you at the Orange Lantern Inn at two."

"I'll be there."

Tony drove back to the office where Mindy was still working on the license plate file. "Anything worthwhile turn up?"

"Not yet, but I haven't started cross-referencing the original sheets. As usual, most of the plates have turned up several times each."

* * *

Tony walked into the Orange Lantern Inn at two o'clock on the button. A big guy in his forties with a face like a catcher's mitt was drinking a draft beer and eating one of those Polish sausages that came in a gallon jar.

"You Kennis?" asked Tony, With his mouth full, Kennis nodded. Tony flashed his ID. "First I'll tell you what I got so you see where I'm coming from." Tony ordered a beer for himself and signaled the barkeep to back up Kennis, while fingering a fresh pack of Luckies. He tore off the opening tab and tapped the pack to force a couple of cigarettes out and offered one to Kennis. He lit them both with his Zippo and went on to describe who his client was and the progress of the investigation, that six of the jurors were now identified and four of them were dead. He also mentioned that he advised the two living jurors to get out of town for a while.

"I'm not a big fan of coincidence. I'll admit it can happen, but I think most coincidences ain't coincidences at all. I definitely think you're onto something here," said Kennis. "I'm gonna re-open the Geiger case."

"What can you tell me about it?"

"I never was too happy about it. The husband came home after bowling. Found his wife hanging in the shower. He cut her down, but she was dead. He called us. The Medical Examiner said she'd been dead for three hours. His alibi was waterproof. There was a note written on a portable typewriter that wasn't signed. Their only son was away at college. None of the neighbors saw a god damned thing." Kennis signaled for another round of beers. "The husband didn't buy the suicide thing and frankly, neither did I, but there was nothing to go on. After a couple of weeks the Chief told me to wrap it up. The fact that she was a juror never came up. I can only guess it never occurred to the husband to mention it."

"I'd like to talk to the husband...and take a look at the house. You don't mind, do you?"

"Hell, no. I'd like to go with you, if that's okay. I wouldn't want to cramp your style."

Twenty minutes later, they pulled up in front of the Geiger house in two cars. They hadn't called. Tony had told Kennis he was willing to trade off a wasted trip now and then to see the interviewee's reaction face to face. Kennis agreed.

In this case, Walter Geiger's face reflected curiosity.

"Mr. Geiger, thanks for seeing us," said Tony after being ushered in. The three men sat in the living room. "You never mentioned to Lieutenant Kennis that your wife had been a juror in the Cassetti trial back in '47."

"Why would I have?"

"I suppose no apparent reason, but from your answer, you're confirming it now?" Geiger nodded. "Well, we've identified six of the twelve jurors, including your wife, and four are dead.

The other three were ruled as accidental deaths but could have been murder. One of the things we're trying to do is find out who the other six jurors are to warn them."

"Well, I don't know who they are. Don't they keep records of that stuff?" asked Geiger.

"Yes, but the assignment judge has refused permission to open the file. Of course, that was with only three dead, he may reconsider now. You have no idea who any of them are?"

"Come to think of it, there was a woman that Kathleen struck up a friendship with. They'd get together now and then for shopping and maybe lunch. I only met her once. She came to the funeral. Don't remember her name."

"Is this her?" Tony showed the diner photo of Malina Bankowski.

"Yeah, that's her. Is she dead too?"

"Not yet. I've warned her to get out of town. Can you think of anyone else?"

"I don't even know that I ever knew any names and it's been years. I'll think about it. If anything strikes me, I'll let you know."

"You were never satisfied with the suicide finding, were you?" asked Kennis.

"No, I wasn't. I told you that. First, I just don't think Kathleen would ever commit suicide. Like any married couple, we had our ups and downs, but by and large, she was a happy woman with a good life. Second, that typewriter thing. Why would she do that? If she had wanted to write a message, she would have written it by hand. The suicide finding was pure bullshit. I'm not blaming you, Lieutenant, but it was bullshit. I had the feeling you thought so, too."

"How old was she?" Tony asked.

"Forty-four."

"What about her height and weight?"

"Kathleen was 5-5 and weighed maybe 125 or 130."

"Have you got a photo of her that's maybe five or six years old? About the time of the trial."

"Yeah, I suppose so. What's it for?"

"Routine investigating. People might not remember her name but recognize her picture. I may want to talk with you again. Oh, yeah, scribble your name, address and phone numbers where I can reach you if there's anything further. Here's my card if you think of something later." Geiger completed the task and handed Tony back his notebook.

"I would also like to borrow the funeral parlor sign-in register. You've got it, right?"

"What do you want with that?" asked Geiger.

"I know it seems unlikely that the killer would come to the wake and sign in, but it's worth checking," said Tony.

Outside, Tony and Kennis agreed to share information and went their separate ways.

* * *

Back at the office, Tony called Brendan Cavanagh.

"We're up to four deaths and six jurors," Tony said. "This last one was ruled a suicide. A woman named Geiger who supposedly left a note but it was written on a typewriter and not signed. And another woman responded to the ad I ran. She was a juror. Like I did with the other guy, I told her she should get out of town for a while."

"When did the so-called suicide happen?"

"Last June. I interviewed her husband and the police lieutenant who handled the case. He's re-opening it."

"What's next?"

"Tomorrow, Mindy McCall is going to Bridgeport, Connecticut to speak with a Steven Kilmurray. He changed his name, but he's the son of Harry Cassetti. There's another son, but it looks like he's been in Korea since last winter."

"Any chance you'll get the court records opened to find out who all the jurors were?"

"The assignment judge refused when there were three deaths. Maybe he'll reconsider with four. I'm not going to ask him again. I'll have a friend who's a detective on the State Police do it. Judge Huber will be more likely to respond to an official request."

FIFTEEN

Monday, October 19, 1953, 10:30 A.M.

Mindy parked in front of 1853 Stratford Avenue, Bridgeport, Connecticut - It was a neatly kept turn-of-the-century two-story house.

A woman in her middle forties answered the door.

"Good morning. Are you Mrs. Kilmurray?" Mindy asked.

"Yes, can I help you?"

"My name is Mindy McCall. I'm a private investigator from Hackensack." Mindy displayed her credentials and Mrs. Kilmurray studied them for several moments. "I would like to have a word with you and also with your nephew. I understand he lives with you."

"Yes, he does. But he's not up yet. He works nights. What's this about?"

"I'll be happy to tell you, but it's a little detailed. Nothing for you or Steven to be worried about, though."

"Well, you better come in," said Mrs. Kilmurray, holding the door open. "How about a cup of coffee?"

"That would be nice, thank you." Mrs Kilmurray poured

out two cups and placed the milk and sugar on the kitchen table. Then she walked to the base of the stairs.

"Steven! Come on down. There's someone here to see you!" she yelled.

A few minutes later, Steven, in a bathrobe, hair mussed and a dark shadow on his jaw, ambled into the kitchen. Steven took a long look at Mindy and said, "Aunt Rose, if you'd have told me what she looked like, I would've shaved." He grinned at Mindy.

"Yeah, you're cute too, but I'm here on business. Let me fill you both in on what has happened." Mindy gave them a brief overview of the case.

"My God, that's terrible," said Mrs. Kilmurray. "They just did what they thought was right. We all thought Harry was guilty. Why shouldn't they have thought it?"

"Can you help me identify any of the remaining six jurors?" asked Mindy.

"I can't," said Steven. "I never knew any of their names. I didn't go to the trial. By that time I was living up here with Aunt Rose. What were the names of the ones who've been killed?"

"Kathleen Geiger, Norman Jackson, Charles Jenkins and Marcy Cavanagh."

"Marcy Cavanagh? Are you sure?" asked Steven.

"Yes, I'm sure."

"When was that?"

"May."

"I know her, or, I guess, knew her. She and her husband have a cabin next door to my Aunt Patricia in Sunrise

Lake."

Mindy stiffened up and leaned forward in her chair."Wait! Are you telling me that your aunt's next door neighbor was a juror in the murder trial of her own brother?"

"If you're tellin' me that Marcy was one of the jurors, then that's what I'm tellin' you. Yes.

Patricia is my father's sister. You've met her, Aunt Rose. Remember?"

"Yes, vaguely. I met her at your parents' wedding and then at a funeral but that's been fifteen or twenty years. And she lives next door to one of the jurors? Wouldn't that have disqualified this Cavanagh woman?"

"Yes, it would. If it was known. It probably wasn't known," said Mindy.

"Mrs. Cavanagh was real nice. When we visited one summer, she included the three of us - my brother, my cousin and me - when she took her kids on an ice cream run."

"What a small world," said Mrs. Kilmurray.

"Steven, what's Aunt Patricia's married name?" asked Mindy.

"Zipoli."

SIXTEEN

At a few minutes past noon, Tony slid into a booth at the Route 17 Diner. New Jersey Trooper Detective Pete Lionetti was already seated. They ordered coffee and sandwiches, and then Tony brought Pete up to date with his investigation.

Tony and Pete referred to themselves as cousins but that was not actually the case. Close, but not quite blood cousins. Tony's Uncle Enzo Petrone was married to Luciana Lionetti, who was Pete's aunt. Enzo and Luciana's children were first cousins to both Pete and Tony, who were both born in the same month in 1924 and grew up just two blocks from each other. The boys started school together, graduated from Hackensack High in 1942 and promptly joined the Army and volunteered for the 101st Airborne Division to be dropped into France on June 6, 1944—D-Day.

Paratroopers are basically infantrymen. They simply have a different mode of transportation to get them into a combat zone. Once they hit the ground, there is no difference.

Tony and Pete always got a chuckle watching a World War II movie that depicted paratroopers sitting side by side in a C-47—often called a gooney bird—chatting with one another. The roar of the engines drowned out all conversation. One of Tony's prized memories was Pete tapping him on the shoulder just as they were about to leap into the black night over Normandy in the very early hour morning of June 6th. Pete exaggerated his lip movements so that Tony could get the message:

"It's show time."

"So what do you want from me?" asked Pete.

"Judge Huber gave Mindy the bum's rush when she asked him to unseal the court records. I was hoping you could talk your captain into writing a letter to the judge asking that he do so. There were only three known deaths when Mindy asked. Now there's four. Also, it would be a written request, not a verbal that he could later deny having heard."

"Well, I'll give it a try, but I can't promise anything. But something else occurred to me. When you put that ad in the paper, you likely alerted the killer that the separate so-called accidental deaths had something in common - all former Cassetti jurors. And therefore, they weren't accidents at all."

"Yeah," said Tony, "I'll buy that. So?"

"Well, up to now, he had to go to some lengths to make each death look like an accident, or in the Geiger case, a suicide. The whole idea was to keep someone from making the connection. But now that he probably knows someone has made the connection, all he has to do is kill the ones that are left. It's a lot easier to do that than to stage it to look like something else."

"I thought that was a risk that had to be taken. But I'm

thinking we have a little bit of time. Almost two weeks," said Tony.

"What makes you think that?"

"I'm betting we'll find two more jurors who died in July and August. Cavanagh in May, Geiger in June, Jackson in September and Jenkins in October."

"Why would anyone do that?"

"One reason is to space it out, so it would be less likely to connect them."

"Which you have undone with your ad. We better not count on the guy waiting now. Thanks for lunch, I gotta be gettin' back."

"Call me if the captain won't write the letter, and I'll do it myself. It would be better coming from a police official, but I'll do it if he won't."

* * *

At half past two, Tony took a call in the office from Captain Fergal O'Hea, commanding officer of the Paramus New Jersey State Police Barracks.

"Donohoo, what I want to know is how thorough was your investigation on these four people who have died."

Tony gave him the details. Captain O'Hea seemed particularly interested in the Geiger case and that Lieutenant Charlie Kennis was re-opening it.

"I'll talk to Kennis. I know him from way back. If he backs you up, I'll get the letter hand-delivered to Judge Huber this afternoon. You'll get a copy in the mail."

SEVENTEEN

At six-thirty, Tony and Mindy sat in the dining room of the Yellow Front Saloon. Sheena, the waitress, had taken their orders for a Schlitz and Pabst Blue Ribbon, respectively and the Saloon's special, sliced fillet mignon on toast with onion rings, thick French fried potatoes and a garden salad, served with four dressings in a stainless steel caddy.

"So get this," said Mindy, "and hold onto your hat."

"I'm all ears."

"Mrs. Zipoli, the next door neighbor of the Cavanaghs in Sunrise Lake, is none other than the sister of the late Harry Cassetti. Her maiden name was Patricia Cassetti."

"No kidding? How did that come about?" asked Tony.

"When I mentioned the names of the dead jurors, Steven Kilmurray recognized the name of Marcy Cavanagh. He hadn't known that she was on the jury nor did he know that she had died. He knew her from when he was a child. He and his brother occasionally spent a week or so up at the lake as guests of their aunt. He recalled Marcy taking them all for ice cream."

"That would disqualify her as a juror."

"Only if it came up. It must not have come up," said

Mindy.

"This can't wait. Save my seat. I'm gonna make a quick phone call." Tony entered his office through the bookcase door and dialed a number.

"Hello."

"Brendan, this is Tony Donohoo. Can you tell me the maiden name of Mrs. Zipoli up at the lake?"

"Her maiden name? Why are you asking that?"

"Do you or don't you know her maiden name?"

"I have no clue," said Brendan.

"Would you be surprised if I told you it was Cassetti?"

"Cassetti? My God, was she related to…"

"His sister. Now, do you think Marcy knew that?"

"Absolutely not. She would have mentioned it. And if she knew, she could have gotten off the jury, which would have pleased her. Hell no, she didn't know. How did you find that out?"

"My operative, Mindy McCall, interviewed Cassetti's younger son and he recognized Marcy's name but he didn't know she had been a juror nor that she was dead. He never attended the trial of his father. What I don't yet know is whether Mrs. Zipoli knew that Marcy was on the jury. I called you first. I'm gonna check her out tomorrow. Their year-round house is in Dumont.

"While I've got you," Tony added, "I'm pretty sure that the Paramus State Police Barracks Commander is writing a letter asking Judge Huber to unseal the court records."

"Well, let me know."

"Will do. Good night."

Sheena was serving the steak sandwiches when he returned to the table.

"Thanks, Sheena. I'll have another beer," he said.

"Who'd you call? Cavanagh?" Mindy wanted to know.

"Yeah. He said that Marcy definitely did not know Mrs. Zipoli was Cassetti's sister. He said she would have jumped at the chance to get out of jury duty if she had."

EIGHTEEN

Tuesday, October 20, 1953, 9:00 A.M.

Tony and Mindy sat down in the office with the license plate files. On the blackboard, they wrote the names of all the victims, the living jurors, the prosecuting and defense attorneys and Judge Willcox. Next to each name was inserted the license plate number that each person used.

"Let's keep it simple," said Tony. "Let's just take the cards we have on each plate. Each plate will probably turn up two or three times in the last year. Disregard anything older than that. Then we take out the original lists and see if any other plate was at multiple locations."

"You mean, any plate number of the other jurors, or any plate that turns up repeatedly?"

"Both. We may turn up Ezekial Fussbucket."

"Oh, yes. Good old Ezekial, our unknown suspect."

After an hour of shuffling 3X5 cards, Tony said, "I'm gonna leave you to this important task and run over to the Zipoli home hoping to catch Patricia Zipoli."

Twenty minutes later, Tony knocked on the door of the Zipoli house in Dumont. Mrs. Zipoli answered the door in a house coat. Her face registered recognition, and then displeasure.

"Good morning Mrs. Zipoli. Remember me? Tony Donohoo. I was at your house in Sunrise Lake on Saturday?"

"Yes, I remember you. What do you want?" She didn't smile.

"The other day I told you I was investigating the death of Marcy Cavanagh, but I didn't tell you why. Four people with something in common, of whom Marcy was one, have died in what appears to be accidents or suicide in just the last five months. Can you guess what they have in common?"

"I have no idea. How could I?"

"I'll be happy to explain it to you. May I come in?"

"No, I don't think so. I have no interest in your problem," she said.

"That's okay. I can do it right here."

"I don't want to hear it. Good-bye." She started to close the door, but Tony stuck his foot over the door sill.

"All four of those people were jurors at the trial of Harry Cassetti. And you are Cassetti's sister. Let me ask again. May I come in, or do you want me to continue out here where the neighbors can hear me?"

She swung the door wide and motioned Tony inside.

"Did you attend your brother's trial?"

Mrs. Zipoli had her arms folded across her chest. Nothing approaching a smile had crossed her lips so far.

"I wasn't there for jury selection, but I went the first day there was to be testimony. I was shocked to see Marcy in the jury box. I don't think she saw me and I left immediately."

"Did you inform the prosecutor or the defense attorney that one of the jurors was your next door neighbor?"

"No, I didn't want to be involved. I didn't want to be identified with Harry. I had a married name. There was no need for anyone to know my maiden name."

"Were either of Harry's sons present?"

"No. One was off in the army, and the other moved to Connecticut and took the last name of relatives."

"Did you have have any conversation with Marcy on this subject at any later time?"

"You're not listening. *I didn't want anyone to know!*" she shouted.

"I'm just covering the bases. It's called investigating. If you'd like to keep this a secret, you might want to cooperate with me."

"I'm sorry. What do you want to know?" Her lip quivered.

"Did Marcy know your maiden name?"

"I can't say for certain she never heard it from my husband or my son, or even from me at some point before the murder. But I think it unlikely that she ever heard it and very unlikely if she did that she would remember it. Years back, my nephews would sometimes stay with us for a week or so in the summer. It's possible she heard their last name, but if she did, it doesn't appear that she made the connection."

"Were you close to Marcy?"

"We've always kept any neighbors at arms length to maintain privacy. So, no, we weren't close, but were good neighbors."

"Did you ever have any conversation with Harry Jr. or Steven on this topic at any later time?"

"No, I didn't. I haven't seen either of them since their mother was murdered."

"Did you know any of the other jurors?"

"No."

"Okay, you didn't know them, but did you know any of their names?"

"No."

"Do you hold them responsible for the wrongful execution of your brother?"

"No, the jury probably acted in good faith, but I do hold the judge responsible for giving the death penalty when he could have sentenced Harry to a long prison sentence. If he had, Harry would be out and about right now."

"At that time, did you think Harry was innocent?"

"Innocent is a peculiar word to describe Harry. He was hardly innocent. He had a bad temper and a mean streak going back to when we were kids. It turned out he didn't kill his wife, but he was cruel and physically abusive to her and to the boys. So, no, I didn't think he was innocent. I wouldn't have lifted a finger to see him convicted, his being my brother, but the same is true of getting him off. Not that there was an opportunity for me to get him acquitted. I suppose I could have gone to his attorney and volunteered some character reference testimony, but it wouldn't have held water and besides, then it would come out that I was his sister."

"Did you kill any of the jurors?"

"Certainly not! How can..."

Tony cut her off with upraised hands. "Covering the bases, that's all. Do you know who killed any of the jurors?"

"Okay," she said, once again holding her temper in check. "No I don't."

"Did it occur to you that Marcy's drowning death was connected to her jury service?"

"Never entered my mind. Now let me ask you a question. As a policeman, are you required to put my name on some report saying I was Harry's sister?"

"I'm not a policeman. I'm a private investigator."

"You told us you were a policeman up at Sunrise Lake."

"I did not. I told you I was a New Jersey State Detective, which I am. Here's my I.D. and shield. And here's my card, if you later want to contact me."

"If you're a private detective, who's paying you? Who's your client?"

"That's confidential."

"Oh, so that's confidential. What about me? Can you keep it confidential about me?"

"I'm not going down to the local gin mill and talk it up, but if it later proves to have some bearing on the case, then it will come out. Also, I may call on you again and expect your co-operation if I do. Otherwise, it won't come from me."

"How did you find out, anyway?"

"An operative of my agency interviewed your nephew up in Bridgeport. When he heard the name Marcy Cavanagh, he mentioned that she lived next door to his aunt and uncle in Sunrise Lake. He wasn't blabbing. It's apparent with his name change, he doesn't want to be known as Harry's son, so I'm sure he can relate to your wishes. Why don't you reach out to him and have a talk?"

* * *

Mindy was still working on the license plate file when Tony returned.

"Come up with anything?" Tony asked.

"It's hardly conclusive, but one plate number - BJS 344 - was in the same place as Kathleen Geiger twice and once for Norman Jackson."

"I'll call it in and see who turns up." Tony walked through the bookcase door asked Frankie for change of a dollar. He left the bar to use a pay phone down the street. Then he called a special number that was usually changed twice a year: New Jersey Department of Motor Vehicles. The number was reserved for police officers and on the off chance that the call was traced, Tony didn't want it to come back to him. A cooperative Hackensack cop with five kids knew there was a C-note in it for him to give Tony the new number when it changed.

"DMV."

"Detective Joseph Marcella, Paterson PD, Shield 467," lied Tony. "Owner, make, model, address of BJS 344."

"Hang on." Ninety seconds later, the call resumed: "1949 gray Chevy two-door, Victor Landsman, last known address 126 Sylvan Avenue, Leonia, New Jersey."

"Whatdya mean 'last known address'?"

"The guy's dead. Reported dead to us August 14th."

NINETEEN

"It's a dead end, Mindy. The guy died last summer - before Charlie Jenkins or Norman Jackson. I don't like coincidences, but I suppose it happens," said Tony.

"We still only have half the jurors," said Mindy. "Maybe something else will turn up."

The phone rang, and Tony picked it up.

"Tony Donohoo, New Jersey State Detective"

"It's Pete."

"Oh, hi, Pete, what's up?"

"Somebody took a shot at that lawyer...Haines. At his house. Fired through the dining room window while he was eating dinner."

"No shit? What's the address" Pete read the address off.

"Huber will have to open the records now. Who's in charge of the investigation?" "McGuirl, County Detectives. Know him?" Pete said.

"Yeah, I know him...wish I didn't...Okay, thanks for letting me know." Tony hung up.

"What's going on?" Mindy asked.

"Somebody took a shot at Haines through his dining room window," said Tony.

"Is it against the law to take a potshot at a lawyer? Just kidding. Did he get hit?"

"No. According to him, he had just dropped his fork and he bent over to pick it up. The bullet sailed over him and got embedded in the wall."

"When was this?"

"Last night at supper time. His wife was in the kitchen. Pete got a teletype on it this morning. I'm going over to Haines' house in Maywood. See what I can find out," said Tony.

"Better check this out first," said Mindy holding out a letter.

> New Jersey State Police
> Paramus Barracks
> 1500 Route 17
> Paramus, New Jersey
> COlfax 2-3800

October 19, 1953

The Honorable Endicott Huber
Assignment Judge of the Superior Court
Bergen County Courthouse
10 Main Street
Hackensack, NJer

Dear Judge Huber:
It has come to my attention that the jurors who served on the Cassetti trial in 1947 may be at risk. Perhaps that is also

THE CASE OF THE DEAD JURORS • 111

true of the attorneys and the judge.

This is a request to unseal the court records to permit us to warn and protect those people. Four of those jurors have died within the last few months with the official ruling being accidental death or suicide. Six of the jurors have been identified as listed below. Please provide my office with the names of the remaining six jurors.

Marcy Cavanagh, accidental death, May
Kathleen Geiger, suicide, June
Norman Jackson, accidental death, September
Charles Jenkins, accidental death, October
Malina Bankowski
Andrew Panzavecchia

It is my belief that all four deaths were as a result of first degree murder. Steps have been taken to warn Mrs. Bankowski and Mr. Panzavecchia to be on their guard and preferably to leave the area until this matter can be thoroughly investigated and brought to a conclusion.

It is my opinion that time is of the essence, and I ask that your office advise

> me by telephone of the identities of the remaining six jurors.
>
> Respectfully yours,
>
> Fergal O'Hea
> Captain
> Barracks Commander
>
> FOH: mt
> bcc: Anthony Donohoo Investigations

Tony read the letter over twice. "That should get Huber off his ass. Especially when he gets wind that Haines is a candidate for Swiss cheese. Anyway, I'm going over to Haines's house. Wanna come?"

"If I'm with you, you're less likely to piss somebody off, so it's probably a good idea," said Mindy.

* * *

Haines' small house was sealed off with several uniformed officers keeping the gawkers away.

Tony flashed his credentials at one officer and asked to see Detective Al McGuirl. McGuirl lumbered his eighth of a ton out to the curb. He glowered at being interrupted.

"What the hell do you want, Donohoo?" he blurted.

In the movies, private detectives are always at odds with the official police. Tony followed his father's advice to try to maintain good relationships with the cops, and he was mostly successful. Mostly. Big Al McGuirl was one of the exceptions. McGuirl like to be called "Big Al." Tony once attended the wake of a cop that McGuirl had worked with. Tony noticed the card affixed to a basket of flowers was signed "Big Al McGuirl."

"I saw Haines last week and warned him he might be at risk. He didn't take me seriously. Four of the twelve jurors in the Cassetti trial back in '47 have taken the stairway to heaven since May. Haines was Cassetti's lawyer."

"Four people dead since May? How were they ruled?"

"Three accidents and a suicide. I think they were all murders. My client is the spouse of one of them."

"Well, four is hard to swallow. Maybe you're right for once," said McGuirl.

"Can I see where the shooting took place?"

"No, you can't. We're still searching for anything that might identify the shooter, or where he stood and we can't have civilians tramping around the crime scene."

"Well, just tell me then. I'm told Haines was in the dining room and someone fired at him through the window, but missed and the bullet lodged in the wall. Is that right?"

"Yeah, that's about it."

"Where is the dining room."

"The back of the house, off the kitchen. Now I gotta get back there," said McGuirl, his voice dripping with impatience.

"Did you find the gun?"

"No gun. .38 slug."

"Is Haines around?" Tony called after McGuirl's retreating figure.

"He's in the house," shouted McGuirl.

"Can one of these guys tell him I want to talk with him?"

"Yeah, go ahead. Just stay the hell out of the way!"

One smiling cop heard the exchange and went through the front door. After a few seconds, the cop returned to the door and signaled Tony and Mindy to come ahead.

Haines and his wife were seated in their living room.

"Come to gloat, Donohoo?" said Haines.

"This is my operative, Mindy McCall. Mindy, Bob and Thais Haines."

Everyone nodded.

"No, not to gloat," said Tony. "To investigate. What time did this happen?"

"Last night about seven. We were eating dinner. Thais got up to get something in the kitchen. I dropped my fork and bent over to pick it up and BANG! I actually heard the bullet whiz past my head. It went into the wall. They dug it out already. Did you ever have anybody shoot at you so you could hear the bullet whiz past?"

"I jumped into France on D-Day. Lots of people shot at me, and yes, I have heard bullets whizzing by. Can I look at where you were sitting?"

"Yeah, come on. But don't actually go in the room."

They walked into the kitchen. Tony stood in the doorway to the dining room. A string was attached to the wall where the bullet lodged, and passed through the hole in the window, on out into the back yard, and eventually fastened to a stick in the ground. The string was taut and straight so that somewhere along the path of that string is where the shooter stood and fired at Haines inside the dining room.

"And where were you when this happened, Thais?"

"I had the fridge open to get more butter. It scared the beejesus out of me. Do you think they'll figure out who did it?"

"I don't know. Last week, Judge Huber refused to unseal the court records, but since then we've come up with another death and now this. It looks like they're not just going after the jurors. Judge Willcox and Notella had better watch themselves also. The State Police have asked Judge Huber to unseal the records. I'm guessing now he'll do it."

"Notella called just before you came in. He's on his way over here. I don't think he needs to be told to be on the alert."

"I saw him last week and told him then," said Mindy. "Did you have any warning that you were in danger?"

"You mean other than Donohoo, right? The answer is no."

"What's alarming about this is the change of method," said Tony. "The four dead jurors were all made to look like accidents, except for one suicide. It's harder and riskier to kill someone and make it look like an accident. The killer did that to keep the authorities from connecting the deaths. But now the killer must know the connection has been made so he justs stands outside a window and blasts away like somebody out of the old west. Billy the Kid in the back yard. When Notella gets here, ask him for protection. You can't keep dropping your fork."

"Why do you say the killer knows the connection has been made?" asked Thais.

"Probably because of the ad I put in the paper asking former jurors to come forth."

"So it's your fault," said Haines with a I-thought-so shrug.

"Yeah, you can blame me if you want, but only after you blame Huber for refusing to release the names of the jurors. By the way, you got a gun?"

"No, I don't have a gun."

"Get one."

The bell rang, and Thais admitted Louis Notella and a detective on the prosecutor's staff. Haines filled them in. Then, Notella called out the window to McGuirl to come in. They huddled in the kitchen for some minutes. Notella came back into the room and noticed Mindy.

"Miss McCall, pleasant to see you again. And this must be Mr. Donohoo?"

"Right again, Mr. Notella."

"You should know that I got a call an hour ago from the chambers of Judge Huber. He unsealed the court records on the Cassetti case insofar as the jurors' names. Unfortunately, I can't give you the names. He specified only official forces."

"I'm glad," said Tony. "At least the other eight people can be warned."

"'Fraid not. Only six."

"Don't tell me. One in July and one in August,"

"Bingo. How'd you know that?"

"We had May, June, September and October. It figured. What was the coroner's cause of death?'

"One was an elderly woman who fell down a flight of stairs, and the other was a guy who asphyxiated himself in his garage with the motor running. Coroner ruled an accident and a suicide, respectively. Now everybody's got to go to work to find out what really happened. You got any leads on who the killer might be?"

"Not really. One clue I can't ignore is who would know who all the jurors were? Mindy and I have been breaking our asses for the last ten days, and we came up with only half of them. But our guy seems to know all of them. How does he know? Could be someone who works in court records. Could be one of the jurors who kept notes. Or it could be Judge Willcox, Judge Huber, you or Haines here."

"Doesn't that hole in the wall take me off your list, asshole?" asked Haines.

"That dropping-the-fork story is a little thin. Judging from your physique, that's probably the first time in years you didn't have a firm grip on your fork.

"Hey, go to your separate corners. C'mon guys, this isn't getting us anywhere," said Notella.

"There's the door, Donohoo. Don't let it hit you on the ass!" Haines said.

TWENTY

"Well, I'm glad I came along to keep you from pissing people off. You're a smooth talker all right," Mindy said once in the car. Her arms were folded across her shapely chest.

"Yeah, I could have handled that better, but Haines rubs me the wrong way."

"And clearly the reverse is true as well."

"Did it occur to you that his story may be bogus?" Tony asked.

"Actually, I must admit it did. I looked out the kitchen window where that string went and he could have stood out there without being seen by a neighbor. Shoot through the window and then run into the house. It would be dark by seven o'clock. If his story is accepted at face value, then it removes him as a suspect. But, if he faked it, I don't think that's the reason. His practice is in the dumps, and this gives him free publicity and stature."

"That's my girl. Mind like a steel trap. Have I told you lately that your brain appeals to me even more than your body, if that's possible?"

"Shut up, Tony. And buy me some lunch."

They grabbed two foot-long hot dogs at Ott's Spot on Route 17, washed them down with a couple of beers, and headed back to the office.

* * *

On arrival, Tony called Pete Lionetti.

"Pete, I understand you got the names of the other six jurors."

"Yeah, we got 'em, but I'm not sure I can give them to you."

"Did the captain tell you that you couldn't?"

"No, he didn't mention it at all."

"Are you guys working on the case?" asked Tony.

"No. McGuirl hasn't asked for help."

"My guess is that he'll concentrate on the two dead jurors that just surfaced - the asphyxiation and the fall down the stairs. My plan is to work the others first, and then go back to the two victims. If I find out I guessed wrong, I'll work it the other way around. Just to stay out of his way, y'know?"

"Look, I don't wanna read these names over the phone. I'll make up a list and give it to you later.

Why don't you meet me at the Route 17 Diner at four o'clock?"

"I'll be there."

"Is he going to give you the names?" Mindy asked.

"I'm meeting him later and he'll give me the list."

Mindy had errands to run and left. Tony grabbed a cup of black coffee and lit up a Lucky from a fresh pack. Alice buzzed him to pick up the phone.

"Tony Donohoo."

"Hi, I called the other day about the ad you ran in the paper."

Yeah, but you didn't leave your name. What is your name?"

"No names right now. Listen, I think I know who's doing the killings."

"You *think* you know who's doing the killings? But you won't tell me who you are."

"Do you want to hear what I have to say or don't you?" asked the caller.

"Shoot. I'm all ears."

"Okay. I've seen this person a bunch of times in the past year. It's kind of weird and a little bit scary because I catch this person looking at me, and then turn away."

"What's this got to do with the Cassetti jurors?"

"It does. That's all I can tell you."

"Listen, if you don't want to talk on the phone, meet with me in some public place."

"All right, I'll meet you at the New Bridge Inn in Riveredge at 7:30."

"7:30 it is. Drinks are on me," said Tony, ringing off.

* * *

Tony rolled into the Route 17 Diner at five to four, took a table and ordered black coffee. When Pete arrived, he slipped Tony a blank envelope which he placed in an inside jacket pocket.

"I got an interesting call a little while ago. I got two responses to my ad in the paper. One was a lady I interviewed who was one of the jurors: Bankowski. I was out when they called in. The other was a guy who said he'd call back but wouldn't leave a name. That was three days ago. He called back. I still don't know his name, but he says he thinks he knows who the killer is. He agreed to meet me at 7:30 tonight at the New Bridge Inn. Wanna come with me?"

"Yeah, I do. But he might not want to talk with a cop. You go in, and I'll wait in the parking lot and take down all the plates for you."

* * *

Pete parked his own car in the lot at the New Bridge Inn by 7:15. Tony arrived at 7:25 and gave just a nod of recognition to Pete as he walked into the bar. Tony took a stool and ordered a bottle of Schlitz. At 7:40, the bartender answered the phone, and called out "Is Tony here?"

"Yeah, that's me.

"This is Tony," he said into the phone.

"I'm not coming."

"Whatd'ya mean you're not coming?....Wait a minute... you've seen something. At least tell me what it was you saw."

"It's probably just a coincidence. I don't want to get involved in this."

"The Cassetti jurors are in danger. If you or someone you

care about was one of them, you're involved big time. What harm can there be in telling me what you saw? I'm not the cops for crissakes."

"No, I'm gonna hang up. I'm sorry I bothered you."

"Wait. The killer knows who you are and you're worried about me? Use your head. Six people are dead. I may be your best chance. Hello...hello...hello...Shit!"

Tony walked out to the parking lot. "Come on in. I'll buy you a beer. The guy called and said he ain't coming. He's got cold feet and doesn't want to get involved. The stupid bastard is afraid of the wrong thing."

"Did he give you any clue as to what he saw? Pete asked as they settled on the barstools.

"Give my friend here a Ballantine," Tony told the barkeep. "Yeah, in the first phone call, he said he had seen someone a number of times. And I think he knows who the person is."

"Wouldn't he have talked to the person if he knew him?" asked Pete.

"Knowing who the person is and knowing him to talk to are two different things. The impression I got, and it's just that—an impression—is that he recognized the person but is not acquainted."

"So what happens now? What's your next move?"

"I'm gonna work my license plate file over with all these new names. Maybe the caller's license plate will turn up with another one more than once."

TWENTY-ONE

Wednesday, October 21, 1953, 8:00 A.M.

Tony parked and walked into the River Edge Diner.

"Good Morning, Josephine. I'll have coffee black and an order of shit-on-a-shingle."

"Creamed chipped beef on toast for pig-mouth." Josephine called through the connecting window to the kitchen. "Don't you ever order anything else?"

"Yeah, sure I do. But it's not something I make myself. And you people have the best S.O.S. in town."

"You were in the army. I thought everybody in the army hated it," said Josephine.

"There were a lot of things about the army I didn't like, but S.O.S. wasn't one of them."

"So you got anything goin', Tony? Any cases?"

"I'm in the middle of one." Tony took Pete's list of jurors out and studied the names.

> Carol McKelvey
> Elizabeth Collins
> Theresa Froumy - "accidental death" August
> Susan Ganley

Donald Nagle - "Suicide" July
Edward Gleason

"Move your crap outta the way, so I can put your plate down. This ain't your office, y'know."

"With that shy, schoolgirl manner, Josephine, it's all I can do to keep from climbing over and taking you on the back counter right on top of the jelly doughnuts," said Tony picking up his notes.

Josephine placed her hands on her ample hips and feigned an angry look. "I'd be too much for you, Tony, and you know it."

"Don't I ever? Gimme some more coffee, please. It tends to slow down my libido."

After finishing, Tony got change for a dollar from Josephine to call Department of Motor Vehicles. With six names to check out, this would be the first of at least three calls. He knew from experience not to overburden the clerk in the DMV with too many names.

As valuable a tool as Tony's license plate file was, it could be misleading. It identified that a certain auto was in a certain place at a certain time, but not who was driving it. Banks rarely gave auto loans to housewives, so even in a two car family, both cars would usually be in the husband's name.

* * *

Back at the office, Tony worked on the license plate file. First, he had to determine all the license plates of those possible victims including both lawyers and Judge Willcox, as well as those who were already victims. Then to extract any cards with those plate numbers for the last year. And then finally to study the lists which were the basis for any given card, and then cross reference all the plate numbers of the victims, potential victims and any other numbers that appeared on more than one list. All of this presented a picture not unlike the tip of an iceberg. If two cards on a given car turned up in twelve months, that meant that on 363 days in that year, the overall file could reveal absolutely nothing about the whereabouts of that subject.

Nevertheless, if two plate numbers appeared at two or more locations, especially if they were different locations, it likely was not a coincidence.

At 10:30, Mindy joined Tony in the effort. After a half-hour, Mindy suddenly started.

"Whoa!" she said. "Remember yesterday, a plate turned up a couple of times. BJS 344. It belonged to a dead guy named Victor Landsman?"

"Yeah. What about it?"

"For a dead guy, he gets around. It's turned up three more times."

"I planned to go the Bureau of Vital Statistics this morning to check out the death certificates on Theresa Froumy and Donald Nagle, our fifth and sixth victims. I'll pick up Landsman's death certificate too. This doesn't make sense."

* * *

For a buck apiece, Tony acquired photostats of the three death certificates. Victor Landsman's death certificate indicated he died on March 23, 1953, two months before any of the murders.

The Bureau of Vital Statistics was in the basement. The County Surrogate's office was on the third floor. Tony took the elevator.

The Surrogate's office had a small area for the public. A counter barred the way to the desks and county workers beyond. Tony stepped up to the counter.

"I'd like to get the name and address of the executor of this man," Tony said placing the death certificate of Victor Landsman on the counter. A thin, gray-haired woman, seemed to resent anyone attempting to avail themselves of public information, ignored the document.

"Take a number first," she ordered, pointing a bony finger at a hook on the wall with cards hanging from it numbered sequentially.

"There's no one else here," Tony pointed out.

"Come back when you've taken a number." The woman probably started the numbering system back when Woodrow Wilson was still a professor at Princeton. Tony walked over and removed the top card.

"Number nine," Tony said, placing it on the counter. The woman, who had walked away from the counter as if Tony's business had been concluded, returned and glanced at the document. Without a word, she left the counter to disappear in the bowels of filing cabinets and returned after several minutes. *Linda Magee, 728 Knickerbocker Road, Cress-*

kill. was written in pencil on a small piece of unadorned notepaper.

"Thank you," Tony said without gaining any response from the woman.

Cresskill was a twenty minute drive from the county hall of records. Number 728 turned out to be a three story Victorian house with a circular driveway. Tony stepped up onto the massive porch and twisted a mechanical doorbell. After a few moments, a woman opened the door. She wore a maid's kit with a starched white pinafore.

"I would like to speak with Linda Magee, please," Tony said while flashing his shield.

The maid nodded and closed the door. After a minute, the maid re-opened the door and asked Tony to come in. She led him into a room that could only be called a parlour. Not a parlor with the American spelling, but parlour with the British spelling. The furniture and wall hangings appeared every bit as old as the house. A candlestick telephone rested on an end table.

"Mrs. Magee will be with you in a few moments," said the maid, and left the room.

Tony was drawn to a brass urn on the mantle of an over sized fireplace. It was engraved:

Patrick Magee
Born: March 17, 1884
Died: June 24, 1951

A woman in her sixties breezed into the room. She didn't smile.

"Good morning, Mrs. Magee. I'm Tony Donohoo, New

Jersey State Detective," as he presented his credentials.

After studying the card and shield for a few seconds, she said: "State your business, young man."

"Yes, ma'am. The county lists you as the executrix of the estate of Victor Landsman. Is that correct?"

"Yes, it is."

"May I ask what your relationship was to Mr. Landsman?"

"I am, or was, his sister."

"Among his property was a 1949 Chevrolet with license plate number BJS 344. The record shows that he died on March 23 of this year and yet that automobile was observed on about a half dozens occasions in the months that followed. Can you explain that?"

"I can't see any earthly reason why I should."

"Mrs. Magee, I am conducting an investigation into what is believed to be multiple homicides. And that vehicle was seen at a number of places at the same time as several of the victims. I would appreciate your cooperation in explaining how a dead man's vehicle was used and who used it."

"That automobile was used by a member of the family for a few months following Victor's death. That person couldn't possibly be involved in multiple homicides."

"And what is the name of that family member, ma'am?"

"The name of that person is none of your affair. Good day to you, Detective."

TWENTY-TWO

Mindy was deep into comparing the license plate files, looking for plate numbers that turned up at the locations of the different jurors, both dead and alive.

"How's it coming?" asked Tony.

"It's coming. What did you find out about Victor Landsman?"

"His sister is the executrix of his estate. She turned out to be an upper crust bitch of the first order. I couldn't get anything out of her."

"Well, I'm going to lunch. Then, I've got an appointment at the *Bergen Evening Record* to pitch some of my photos," said Mindy.

"Hey, while you're there, check out something in the archives for me. Look up the obits for Donald Nagle in May, Theresa Froumy in August and one Patrick Magee, who died June 24, 1951. Get me the names of the relatives listed."

"Who's Patrick Magee?"

"The late husband of Landsman's executrix. I took his death date off the urn that contains his ashes."

"And what are you up to?"

"I'll be interviewing the remaining four surviving jurors. That' includes Elizabeth Collins, Edward Gleason, Carol McKelvey and Susan Ganley."

* * *

First on the list was Elizabeth Collins. She lived in a Tudor style apartment house in Englewood. There was no doorman. Tony entered the lobby and saw "Collins" on the mailbox for apartment 2B. He went up the stairs and rang the bell. While waiting for a response, a teen-aged girl in penny loafers and a ponytail walked toward him with a load of schoolbooks pressed against her chest.

"Are you looking for my mom?" she asked.

"Is your mom Elizabeth Collins?"

"Yes, but she's working."

"I'm Tony Donohoo, New Jersey State Detective," he said, flashing his shield and I.D. "What's your name?"

"I'm Sandy. I'll bet you want to talk to her about that jury thing. Another detective called and told me to tell her to be on the lookout."

"Can you tell me where she works?"

"She's the day manager at the Milestone Restaurant up in Englewood Cliffs, but she wouldn't want to talk to you there. She'll be home about six."

"Okay, Sandy. Give me your phone number, and I'll call her tonight."

Tony's next stop was in Closter. He found the address he was looking for, a sprawling ranch house, not more than two or three years old. The shrubbery had not yet fully matured. Before he could get to the bell, the door opened halfway and a middle-aged woman peered out.

"Can I help you?"

"You can if you're Carol McKelvey."

"And who might you be?"

"Tony Donohoo, New Jersey State Detective." He showed his shield and I.D.

The woman motioned him inside. Only then did Tony notice she had a .38 police special in her right hand. She wore a skirt, blouse and sweater. Tony took the chair she pointed to, and she sat on the sofa with a coffee table between them.

"You're State Police?" she asked. Normally people inferred State Police, but she wanted confirmation.

"No, I"m a private detective. Here's my card."

"Who hired you?"

"Sorry. Confidential at this time. I gather you've been warned about the other jurors."

"Yeah, I got a phone call from the office of the county prosecutor," she said.

"No one's been to visit you?"

"No, just a call."

"Is it Miss or Mrs.?"

"Mrs."

"Okay, let me get to it. There were twelve of you and there's six left. All the others were staged to look like accidents or suicides but that was to prevent anyone from connecting the deaths. If you think about it, it's a lot harder to kill someone and make it look like an accident than just to shoot them. Speaking of shooting, do you wanna put the cannon down now?"

"No, I don't. My husband told me to keep it on me at all times and especially if someone came to the house. I'm not pointing it at you, so live with it."

"Okay, you win. I got two missions. One is to warn the former jurors that they are at risk, and you've been so warned. The second is to find the killer."

"Why you? Why not the police?" Mrs. McKelvey set the pistol down long enough to take a filtered cigarette out of a silver box on the coffee table. Tony popped out a Lucky and fired up his Zippo. He reached across to light hers, but she put up a stop sign with her hand and picked up the revolver again. Then she used the silver Ronson on the coffee table.

"I got in this before they did. Through the efforts of my agency, we convinced the cops that the deaths were connected, but we only knew about four of them. Theresa Froumy and Donald Nagle we didn't find out about until the judge unsealed the records. I want you to go back six years and tell me what you can about the other jurors. I mean, last week, could you have told me any of their names?"

"No, not full names. Maybe one or two I could remember the first name."

Tony spread the six photos on the coffee table. "These four are dead. These two are still living."

"I remember this guy," she said pointing to the picture of Charlie Jenkins. "He was arrogant. Not a nice man. He sort of bullied anyone who didn't go for guilty right away."

"How long were you in sequestration?"

"We were charged right after lunch. We were in the jury room until about nine o'clock, with a dinner break in between, but we didn't leave that room until they escorted us to the hotel."

"Recognize anybody else?"

"This girl. I should say woman. Pretty. She was in her thirties. She was outspoken but likable, you know? This is her," indicating Marcy Cavanagh's photo.

"How outspoken? For the defendant?"

"No, just the opposite. She was adamant that he be found guilty."

"Was there anybody who thought he was not guilty?"

"Oh yeah. A couple of them. This woman—I don't remember her name—was the longest holdout." She was pointing at the picture of Malina Bankowski. "She didn't give any reasons why she thought he was not guilty. She just didn't want to find him guilty. I remember she cried when the judge gave the death sentence."

"When these deaths were reported in the last five or six months, did you recognize any of the names or realize it was one of the former jurors?"

"Nope. Never had a clue until I got a call last night."

"Did you think Cassetti was guilty?"

"I thought he was probably guilty, but the evidence wasn't for sure. I didn't really speak much. I could have gone either way."

"What did you think of the death sentence?"

"I was surprised. So were the other jurors, as best I remember."

"What about this guy?" Tony asked pointing at the picture of Norman Jackson with his wife.

"I don't remember him at all. Nor this one. What is he, a bartender?" Andy Panda's picture showed him in apron and the array of whiskey bottles behind him.

"Yeah, he is. Can you remember this lady?" Tony asked, indicating Kathleen Geiger.

"Yeah, I do. She was for guilty, but she was nice and sympathetic. I recall that she spoke up for the other woman once or twice when some were getting impatient. What did you say? Bankowski?"

"I didn't say. So you do remember her name?

"I guess it just came back to me. Bankowski, that's right, isn't it?"

"Yeah, that's right. The two victims Theresa Froumy and Donald Nagle, I don't have pictures of. Do you remember anything about them?"

"No, I don't recall those names, if I ever knew them." Mrs. McKelvey took a fresh cigarette out of the box and lit it from the one she was smoking. After a few moments, Tony noticed she had not fully extinguished the first one. It continued to smolder in the ashtray and he resisted the urge to reach over and stub it out.

"Walking around with that piece is not a bad idea, but a better one would be to get out of town for a couple of weeks. If you do that, please make a collect call to me to let me know how to reach you. Meanwhile, write your name, phone and address in here," Tony said passing over his notebook and pen, She picked up the pen and wrote in the book with her right hand while holding the pistol in her left.

"One last thing and I'll be on my way. I want to take a photo of you to show the other jurors. I have to get my camera out of the car."

"Okay. I'll step out on the porch, and you can take it there. I'll keep the gun out of sight," said Mrs. McKelvey, with a grin.

TWENTY-THREE

"I hope you like my southern fried chicken because that's all you're gonna get tonight. Maybe by the weekend I'll be back in action," Mindy said, while turning the chicken in her fry pan.

Tony relaxed in Mindy's kitchen with a double dry martini and three pimento-stuffed olives. He related his meeting with Mrs. McKelvey.

"I don't blame her, packing a gun," Mindy said. "I'd do the same thing. She trusted you enough to let you in her house but not so much as to lay that pistol down. Pistol packin' mama. By the way, I know you like to sprinkle Tabasco sauce on fried chicken. Get it out of that cabinet."

"According to Carol McKelvey, Marcy Cavanagh, Charlie Jenkins and Kathleen Geiger were all for guilty. She didn't remember Norman Jackson, even looking at his picture. But his wife indicated he was convinced Cassetti was guilty."

"Well, all twelve voted to convict."

"Yeah, but some were more reluctant than others. So how did your day go?" asked Tony.

"I have the obits you asked for. Donald Nagle was 42

and left a wife, Christine and a son and daughter in Rockleigh. Theresa Froumy was 73 and lived in Ridgefield Park. She has a son named Chester Froumy in Teaneck. But there's a big surprise for you. Take a look at that paper on top of my mail on the counter. It's a transcript of an obituary notice from June 27, 1951, for one Patrick Magee. Check out the list of his survivors."

"Holy shit! Thais Haines!" exclaimed Tony. "So she's the one who borrowed the car of Victor Landsman. Do you think she was Landsman's niece as well as Magee's? Who's she related to, Patrick or Linda Magee?"

"I think she was a Landsman because she's listed with two nephews who bear that name. The order of the names implies they're her brothers. But that would make her Patrick's niece by marriage."

"Yeah, how many times did that license plate turn up? Was it five or six times?" asked Tony.

"I think it was six, but you don't know yet that it was her. You're jumping to conclusions."

"That's her! Tomorrow I gotta study exactly who else was there. I wonder if there were any repeats? If she was at the same place with one of the jurors more than once. Once I get that down, I'll hit her with it."

"She and her husband already hate you, maybe I should be the one," Mindy said.

"I'd be worried she'd sit on you with that big fat ass."

"Eat your chicken," Mindy said, putting his plate down. "There's cold potato salad in the bowl."

After dinner, Tony called the number that Sandy Collins

had given him. A woman answered on the third ring.

"Good evening, Mrs. Collins, this is Tony Donohoo, New Jersey State Detective."

"Did you speak to my daughter about this jury thing?"

"No, the only conversation I had with your daughter was limited to how I could reach you. I didn't discuss the case at all. I appreciate your wanting to keep her out of this."

"Well, that cop that called yesterday gave her an earful," said Mrs. Collins. "He must be a moron."

"Look, I'm trying to find the killer. Won't you feel a lot better when that happens?"

"Of course I will."

"Well, then, help me out. Meet with me."

"Can't we just do this on the phone?"

"No, we can't. Mrs. Collins, you are in danger. I'm trying to find the killer before he strikes again. Is it too much to ask you to cooperate with me? Pick a public place to meet with me."

"All right. I'm sorry. How about the Cottage Shoppe in Englewood Cliffs at 10:30 tomorrow morning? That's right down the street from where I work and I'm due in at eleven."

"Terrific. I'll wear a red carnation so you know me."

"Are you kidding?"

"Yes, I'm just kidding...I'll carry a file folder...See you then." Tony put the phone in the cradle.

"She's upset the daughter knows?"

"Yeah. Whoever the cop was that called to warn her, did so before she got home and he laid it out to the daughter.

The Case of the Dead Jurors • 139

She was furious."

"How old is the daughter?"

"About sixteen."

"I can see why she would want to shield her, but it's probably best that the kid knows what's what. She's got eyes and ears, too."

"Anyway, Elizabeth Collins is a manager at the Milestone Restaurant and has to be in about eleven. So I'm meeting her at the Cottage Shoppe, which is right up the street."

"Okay, I'll wash, Tony and you dry. *Arthur Godfrey and His Friends* are on in ten minutes. I want to see it. Arthur fired Julius LaRosa on the air Monday morning."

"Do you think the McGuire Sisters will be on?"

"Shut up, Tony."

TWENTY-FOUR

Thursday, October 22, 1953, 10:00 A.M. - The Cottage Shoppe, Englewood Cliffs, New Jersey

Tony sat at the oval counter with his file folder. A petite and perky blond in her late thirties dressed in skirt, blouse and heels walked in and looked around questioningly. If she ever lost her job at the Milestone, she could surely find employment as a stand-in for June Allyson. Tony raised a hand and she walked toward him. Tony picked up his coffee cup and motioned to a booth. She slid in opposite him.

"You must be Elizabeth Collins. I'm Tony Donohoo. Here's my I.D. Could I order you something? Coffee? Danish?"

"Just coffee, thanks." Tony signaled to the waitress.

"How do you think I can help you?" she asked.

"I want you to look at these seven pictures. Do you know any of these people by name?"

She studied the photos for several seconds. "I can't say I remember the names, but I recognize some of them."

"These four have died in the last few months," said Tony. "The other three are still living. If you don't remember any of the names, then you probably didn't realize they were four of the former jurors when their deaths were reported. Is that right?"

"The first inkling I got of this was Tuesday night when that stupid cop called and spilled the whole thing to my daughter. She told me when I walked in after work."

"Mrs. Collins, I want to ask about your husband. I know it's a personal question but I'm concerned about your safety and wonder about a husband to protect you."

"Call me Liz. I'm a war widow. My husband was killed in a bombing raid over Berlin in 1943. I've never remarried."

"I believe it is crucial for you not to be alone. Given the track record of this killer, only jurors are the targets. Therefore, even being with your daughter is very likely a protection."

"I'll keep that in mind. How long do you think this will go on?"

"Things are falling into place. My guess is that another week or two will tell all," said Tony. "Now, tell me, how were you leaning in the trial. Guilty or not guilty?"

"I didn't like the look of Cassetti, and there was tons of evidence against him, but it really wasn't conclusive. Most of the jurors wanted to convict, and we talked endlessly the first day of deliberation. They put us up in a hotel. When we came back in the morning, those that wanted to convict were more convinced than ever, and the others were not really in favor of acquittal, they just weren't sure, but they weren't as passionate. After a couple more hours, we all voted to convict."

"Do you remember who was who?"

"Do you mean just of these seven. You don't have all the jurors' pictures."

"You make eight. Two of the other four also died recently, for a total of six dead. Do these seven first. Tell me what you remember."

"I remember this woman. She was for guilty, but she wasn't bitter or closed minded. She was civil and intelligent. She wasn't the foreman, but she did the job of foreman more than the guy who was." She indicated Marcy Cavanagh.

"Who was the foreman?"

"I don't remember his name, and his picture isn't here. This guy" she said, tapping a finger on Charlie Jenkins picture, "was a pain in the ass. He also wanted to convict. This one seemed totally confused the whole time. I think his name was Andy something. That's about all that sticks in my mind."

"What's your best guess who might be doing these murders?" Tony asked.

"I have no idea. I know we convicted the wrong guy, but, as a whole, the jury acted properly. I don't think, however, that if we knew the judge was going to put the guy in the electric chair that we would have convicted him. I mean, it wasn't for certain, you know?"

"Please write your address, home and work numbers where I can reach you," Tony said passing over his notebook. She complied.

With her permission Tony photographed her and she left

for work.

* * *

Tony stayed and had a burger and fries at the Cottage Shoppe. It was high noon when he pulled up in front of Haines' house in Maywood.

"What in hell do you want?" asked Thais Haines when she answered the doorbell. "Bob isn't here. He's at the office."

"I didn't come to see Bob. I came to see you."

"What about?"

"Before we get to that, may I come in?"

"No, tell me what you want first."

"I want to talk to you about your late uncle, Victor Landsman."

"How do you know he was my uncle?

"I'm a detective. It's my job to find things out. You used his car for several months after he died.

Are you going to ask me in, or should I just go to Notella's office and explain it to him."

"I can't see why Notella would be interested in my uncle's car. Oh, all right, come in, but I don't have all day. So I used my uncle's car after he died. What's that to you?"

They sat in the living room. Thais lowered herself into an easy chair more gracefully than he would have guessed. She was a big woman, but not really fat. Big boned, at least five-eight.

"What did you think of the jury? Do you think they acted

in good faith?"

"Is that what you came here to ask me?"

"Yes, and I have a few other questions." said Tony.

"Did they act in good faith? Well, no. Not if you apply reasonable doubt. They either didn't understand the concept or chose to ignore it. But if you're getting around to suggesting that I felt so strongly about it that I'd go around bumping them off one by one, you're chasing your own tail."

Tony produced his pack of Luckies. "Do you mind if I smoke?"

"Yes, I do mind. You're not gonna be here long enough to smoke it," Thais said, folding her arms across her chest. Tony put the cigarettes back in his pocket.

"Your uncle's car turned up six different times between April and August in the same place as four different people who were jurors on the Cassetti trial. Two of those people are now dead. Your aunt, Linda Magee, told me a family member used that car for a few months after Uncle Victor died in March. She wouldn't tell me who, but I figured it out. Why did you borrow a car in the first place? Why not use the car in the driveway?"

"I only bought it in August, secondhand. How can you possibly know where some car was on some date?"

"I have to keep reminding you that I'm a detective. When I or any of my operatives are on the job, we routinely take down all the other license plate numbers at any location that our subject visits."

"You were following these potential murder victims around before they were murdered? Or were you following me?"

"Neither. Our reason for being at any of these locations was unrelated to this case," Tony explained.

"So when and where were these visits?"

"All right." Tony produced a list. "You were at the Bowl-A-Rama on Route 17 in Rochelle Park at the same time as Kathleen Geiger. April 22 and May 13."

"Those were Wednesdays, right?" Thais asked, but didn't wait for an answer. "I know that because that's my bowling night. I'll just take a wild guess that it was this Geiger woman's bowling night also."

"So, do you know Kathleen Geiger?"

"Not by name. Maybe by sight, if she hasn't changed too much in the six years. I attended the trial and watched the jury's reaction very carefully. I took notes to help my husband. I used numbers to describe different jurors, not their names. Never knew the names."

"On May 23, you were at Sears Roebuck in Hackensack at the same time as Norman Jackson, who is now deceased."

"Yeah, so sue me. Everybody's got to be somewhere and apparently, that's where I was at the time. What does that mean, besides absolutely nothing?"

"On April 30, you were at the Milestone Restaurant in Englewood Cliffs when another former juror, Elizabeth Collins was there. And on Sunday, June 28 and Monday August 10 you were at Holly's Restaurant and Arnold Constable Department Store respectively at the same time as Edward Gleason. Can you explain that?"

"Yes, I can. But I don't have to, because everything you've said is pure bullshit. The answer to all this is 'so what.' Now get the hell out of my house."

"Your husband lost an appointment to the superior court over this case. Are you still bitter about not being the wife of a judge?"

"Get out and stay away from me and my husband."

As Tony left, he took down the plate number of the '51 blue Plymouth in Haines's driveway.

* * *

"It didn't go too well. She threw me out of the house. She's smarter than I thought. Smarter than her husband. And she doesn't get rattled."

"I told you I should be the one to interview Thais," said Mindy. "If there's a next time, I'm going, not you."

"What have you been doing this afternoon?"

"Going over the funeral parlor guest books that you collected. I've been looking for names that were on more than one book, but I haven't found any. The murderer would have to be a complete moron to sign in with his or her real name. What I didn't try to do was to look for similar handwriting. Before I do that, I have a better idea. We visit the surviving spouses and ask them to go over all the entries and indicate which ones they don't know. That should narrow the search down considerably," Mindy said. "But let's wait until we can get our hands on the books for the other two victims."

"*If* we can get our hands on those books," said Tony.

"I got one already," said Mindy. "I met with her son, Chester Froumy in Teaneck earlier today. He's an only child and the closest relative of Theresa Froumy. She'd been a widow for over ten years. Chester said she was 72 and died from injuries sustained when she fell down a full flight of stairs in her house. She lived alone. Chester found her body. She had been dead about 24 hours. He got worried when she didn't answer the phone. He said she was in excellent health. Did her own housekeeping and still drove a car."

"Did you ask if he knew what she thought about Cassetti being guilty or not?"

"I did. He quoted her. 'That rotten bastard ought to fry in hell.'"

TWENTY-FIVE

At four-thirty, Tony pulled up in front of an old frame two story house in Little Ferry. Tony and Mindy went to the door. A young woman in blue jeans answered the bell.

"Good afternoon. Are you Mrs. Gleason?" asked Tony.

"Yes, can I help you?"

"I'm Tony Donohoo, and this is Mindy McCall. We're private detectives."

"Is something wrong?"

"Yes, I'm afraid there is something wrong," said Mindy. "May we come in?"

"Oh, sure. Come on in." She led them into the kitchen at the back of the house and offered chairs at the table. "What's this all about? Has something happened to my husband?"

"No, no, it's nothing like that, Mrs. Gleason—" began Tony.

Mrs. Gleason exhaled in relief. "Just call me Toni Ann. My real name's Antoinette, but that sounds so stuffy."

"Okay, Toni Ann, we know that your husband was a juror on the Cassetti trial jury back in '47. Is he at home?"

"No, he's due home from work. What about the jury? Ed

and I only got married last year. He's never mentioned being on a jury."

"There were twelve people, and six of them have been murdered in the last few months. They convicted this man Cassetti of murdering his wife and a couple of years later, it was discovered that he was not guilty. And now it looks like somebody is taking revenge. There's also a report that somebody fired a couple of shots at the lawyer who defended Cassetti."

"Oh, my God. I didn't know anything about this. I saw something in the paper about it, but I didn't know that Ed was one of the jurors."

"Toni Ann, I'm home," came a yell from the front of the house. "Who's got the blue Ford out front—"

"That's mine, Mr. Gleason. I'm Tony Donohoo, New Jersey State Detective. This is Mindy McCall, an operative in my agency."

Gleason's face fell. After a moment, he smiled, but it was not a smile of mirth but of embarrassment, and he looked at his wife with an expression of shame. "Honey, I'm sorry. I didn't want you to worry."

"You and I have spoken before, Mr. Gleason. And you broke our date at the New Bridge Inn. I recognize your voice."

"What's he talking about, Ed?" asked Toni Ann.

Ed just looked at her, so Tony took over. "Your husband saw an ad I ran in the *Record* warning the former jurors that they were at risk. He called me but refused to give his name. He told me he thought he knew who the killer was and agreed to meet me to discuss it. But then he called me and said he wasn't coming."

Ed Gleason took his suit jacket off and loosened his tie. He sat at the table with the other three and gave a sigh of relief. "I guess it's a good thing you're here. I don't mind telling you this has been worrying me, but I didn't want to jump the gun. I didn't want to accuse somebody if I wasn't sure."

"Ed, you seem like a bright guy," said Mindy, "but that's just stupid. If you're right in your suspicion, we might be able to keep this creep from killing more jurors, and that includes you!"

"I can't argue with that. Okay, for the last year or so, I have seen this person - I don't know - maybe five or six times at all sorts of different places. And then when I saw your ad, I began to think that, maybe..."

"Was the person connected with the trial?" asked Tony.

"Yes. It's not somebody I know, but I know who she is."

"She? It's a she?"

"For cryin' out loud, Ed, tell them who it is," exclaimed Toni Ann, with frustration.

"It's the lawyer's wife. The guy who defended Cassetti. She's a big broad - looks like a lady wrestler."

"But you don't know her."

"I don't even know her name. I've forgotten the lawyer's name, but I know she's his wife. There was a picture of the two of them coming out of the courthouse in the paper. Right when the trial ended."

"You're sure it's the same woman?" asked Mindy.

"Yeah, she's got one of these faces, you know, that once you've seen her, it kinds of sticks. It's her, no question."

"That's it?" said Tony. "So you've seen this woman. So what?"

"You kinda had to be there. Every time, she's lookin' at me. And when I catch her at it, she looks away. It gave me the creeps even before I saw your ad. I thought this amazon was giving me the evil eye, you know?"

Tony then changed the subject and questioned Ed about how he was leaning during the sequestration and what he remembered about other jurors.

"I hadn't made my mind up. Maybe half of them were sure about convicting. I thought he was probably guilty but the proof was skimpy. The big deal was the gun with his fingerprints. But I could see a guy coming home and finding his wife dead and picking up a gun that was on the floor. He was the one who called the police and had he shot her, he would have wiped the gun clean or gotten rid of it altogether. I was shocked when the judge gave him the chair. I've thought about this a lot since that mob guy confessed."

In preparation of leaving, Tony gave last minute advice. "Now that it's been outed, it's a little more difficult for the killer in one sense but a whole lot easier in another. It no longer has to look like an accident. I'm sure I don't have to tell you to watch your ass. Stay with other people. Your wife, co-workers, anybody. Write down your work and home numbers and your address for me. I'm gonna take your picture before I go. Take my card and let me know if anything else pops into your mind. If it's possible, I suggest the two of you should get out of town for a week or two. Make it a second honeymoon. And when you do, call me collect and let me know how to reach you."

As she escorted Tony and Mindy to the door, Toni Ann whispered: "Thank you."

* * *

Being in the neighborhood, Tony and Mindy went for dinner at Tracey's Nine Mile House in Little Ferry. The place opened in the 1930's, and it got its name from being 8.9 miles from the new George Washington Bridge. The Eight Point Nine Mile House didn't really roll off the tongue. The Nine Mile House was famous for open steak sandwiches served on platters the size of manhole covers with a ton of French fries and onion rings, and a monkey dish side of cole slaw.

Tony and Mindy led off with a couple of dry martinis and ordered the specialty of the house.

"So what do we do now about Thais Haines?" asked Mindy.

"I don't know. I wish I'd known about this before I went there today. I could never get back into her house again, and I'm sure we'll hear from Bob Haines tomorrow. He'll be wailing like a stuck banshee and threatening to sue. I can see her shooting a hole in the wall but killing six people, that's something else."

"Let's get on something important. We can see *Roman Holiday* at the Park Lane Theater in Palisades Park, or *Shane* at the Fox in Hackensack. What's your vote?" asked Mindy.

"That's Gregory Peck and some boyish girl, right?"

"Audrey Hepburn, no relation to Katherine. She's got no boobs so you don't like her. End of story," said Mindy.

"You're right on the money. Let's go see Alan Ladd."

* * *

On the drive back to Tony's apartment, Mindy commented: "I thought the best part of the movie was when that old mongrel dog slinked out of the saloon just before the gunfight between Alan Ladd and Jack Palance. I wonder how they got the dog to do that? He looked at Ladd and then Palance and got up and quietly made his way across the barroom and under the swinging doors."

"Why in hell did they cast Jean Arthur as the wife? She's been around forever. I bet she's over fifty," said Tony. They should have gotten somebody a lot younger."

"And with big boobs, right Tony?"

TWENTY-SIX

Friday, October 23, 1953 - 900 A.M.

"I'm going to work on the funeral guest register books," said Mindy. "I'll call Beatrice Jackson, Brendan Cavanagh, Gertrude Jenkins, and Walter Geiger, and try to meet with each of them today, or even tonight."

"McGuirl's had the names of the other two victims, Donald Nagle and Theresa Froumy, for three days now," Tony said. "I'm sure by now, their spouses have been interviewed, so I'm gonna give them a shot. Also, there's a former juror named Susan Ganley. I'll try to reach her."

First stop for Tony was the home of Christine Nagle in Rockleigh. The post-war split level was just one lot from the New York State line. *If Donald Nagle had bought a house just 100 feet further north, he wouldn't have been a Bergen County resident and not called for jury duty. He'd be alive today.*

A whining vacuum cleaner sounded as he approached the front door. No answer to the doorbell. He figured it couldn't be heard while the vacuum was running. He waited until the sound died out, some three or four minutes, and tried again. Mrs. Nagle was an attractive brunette of about forty, shapely but with a few more pounds than necessary. Her dark hair was tied up with an Aunt Jemima rag. She wore jeans and a blouse.

After introductions and credential display, she invited Tony in.

"Would you like coffee? I have a pot on."

"Yes, thank you, Mrs. Nagle." They sat in the kitchen.

"Are you here to follow up on Detective McGuirl's investigation?"

"No, I'm working independently. I know your husband was on the Cassetti jury, but I have a few questions that I hope are not too repetitive of what has already been covered."

"I feel like such a mess. I've been cleaning all morning. But go ahead, ask away."

"I think you look just fine. Very fine."

Mrs. Nagle gave a coquettish smile.

"What was your husband's occupation."

"Mechanical engineer. He worked at Bendix Aviation in Teterboro."

"Did he talk much about the trial?"

"Oh, yeah. I was very curious and asked him loads of questions. He was the foreman of the jury and gave it to me blow by blow."

"Did he elaborate on the other jurors? Mention any of them by name?

"I think he probably talked about them, but I don't recall him mentioning any names. Mainly he talked about his participation. He said there were some holdouts that caused them to stay overnight. By the next day, of course, they all voted to convict."

"What was his position on whether Cassetti was guilty or not?"

"Don was sure Cassetti did it. Of course, it was all over by the time he could tell me about it. He said Cassetti wasn't a nice guy."

"What about when it turned out that Cassetti hadn't killed his wife? How did he feel then?"

"If you mean did he feel guilty, I don't think so. That was years later, of course. I think he felt the lawyers were to blame. And the judge. He didn't think the judge should have sentenced Cassetti to the death penalty."

"When did he say that? At the time or only after it came out that Cassetti was innocent?"

"No. He said it at the outset that sending the guy to the chair was going overboard."

"I trust you held a wake and funeral for your husband."

"Yes, of course."

"Did you get the guest register from the funeral home? If so, I'd like to see it."

"Give me a minute. Help yourself to more coffee."

After three or four minutes, she returned with the book and handed it to Tony, but he gave it right back to her. Tony handed her a pencil. "I'd like you to go down the list and put an X next to anyone you don't know."

"You don't think the killer came to the funeral, do you?"

"Well, of course, I don't know. You've heard about the killer returning to the scene of the crime, haven't you?" She nodded. "This is a variation of that. Just the ones you don't know. I'll wait."

She began to go down the list. As she did so, she said: "I understand the return to the scene of the crime thing, but do you really think the killer would write his name in the book?"

"Might be an alias," Tony said.

"Nobody made these people sign the book, you know. They could just walk right past it. It would be stupid to sign in."

"Maybe the killer is stupid. We're looking at all the books of the six victims. Something might turn up. It's worth a shot. When you're finished, I want to borrow this book. I'll get it back to you as soon as I can. It will enable us to compare handwriting samples. As I say, we're investigating, and it's worth looking into. By the way, do you have children?"

"Yes. Donald Jr. is 16 and Ruth is 11."

"Did your husband leave you well fixed? Hey, sorry. That's personal. I shouldn't have asked that."

"No, that's all right. He had a sizable insurance policy, and it was double indemnity. After he died, I went to classes and became a real estate agent. We're doing okay."

"By any chance, did you take any pictures of the funeral? Or did you go to a restaurant with those who attended and take pictures there?"

"Ye-e-sss. My son is a camera bug, and he took some pictures in the cemetery. I never thought of them. We didn't go to a restaurant, but I had a small group back here to the house. Maybe he took some shots here also."

"Can you get them for me?"

158 • ROD STERLING

"It might take me a few minutes to find them."

Again she left the room and returned after a spell with the drugstore envelope with a dozen photographs, which she handed to Tony. "I'll leave the prints and just take the negatives if that's all right. I have a darkroom at the office. Tell your boy I'll return the negatives right away. Write your office and home numbers in my notebook, along with your address. I appreciate your help, Mrs. Nagle."

She wrote the information in Tony's notebook. Tony rose indicating departure.

"Keep me posted, and it's Christine," she said.

That was an invitation if I ever heard one, Tony said to himself as he approached the car.

* * *

Nobody was home at the residence of Susan Ganley. A neighbor told Tony that she and her husband ran a delicatessen on Washington Avenue in Bergenfield. It was 11:15 when Tony walked into the deli and asked the man behind the counter for Susan.

"That's my wife," he answered sullenly.

"Tony Donohoo, New Jersey State Detective." He held his I.D. up for the man to see, who reached out to take it. Tony pulled it back. "I'd like to have a word with her. You know about the dead jurors, don't you?"

"Yeah, we heard. This ain't a good time, you know. She's got to get the potato salad ready for lunch time."

"Six of the original twelve jurors have been murdered, Mr. Ganley. I'm trying to find the killer before he gets to

THE CASE OF THE DEAD JURORS • 159

your wife. I think she's more important than potato salad, don't you?"

"Hey Sue," he called out to the back of the store "There's a cop out here wants to talk to you"

A woman appeared from the back wearing a large white apron. She was drying her hands on a towel. "Who are you?" she asked.

Tony introduced himself and displayed his shield. "I'd like to talk to you about your service on the Cassetti jury back in '47. By the way,. I'm not a cop. I'm a private detective. I've been hired by the spouse of one of the murdered jurors. I've interviewed all the living jurors except you. And five of the six family members of the victims. I need about twenty minutes."

"I ain't got twenty minutes."

"If you can't take the time now, then come to my office tonight at seven. Here's my card."

"Yeah, that's better, but I don't know what I could tell ya. What d'ya want to know?"

"Are we going to do it here and now?"

"No, I just figured—"

"Mrs. Ganley, I'm trying to find the killer before he finds you. Why don't you humor me and co-operate. It might just save your life."

"I'll see you at seven then."

"Your husband, or somebody should come with you. Be on the alert. Don't go anywhere alone," Tony added. As he said this, he looked from Mrs. Ganley to Mr. Ganley. They both looked back at him in silence.

TWENTY-SEVEN

Ganley's Delicatessen closed for business weekdays at six, but bank deposits had to be made before three o'clock. Pat Ganley left the bank at 2:55 and strolled back down Washington Avenue, stopping only to buy a couple of packs of Old Golds at the newspaper store across the street from the deli. He lit one on the sidewalk and crossed the street. He walked into the deli and saw a woman waiting by the counter.

"Can I get some service here?" the woman asked impatiently.

"Didn't my wife come out when the bell rang?" He asked pointing to the device hanging over the door.

"No, she didn't. I want a pound of kielbasi and a half-pound of Swiss cheese." Pat tended to the lady's order, and rang up the sale. He then walked into the kitchen area at the back of the store.

Susan Ganley was lying on the floor with a ten inch kitchen knife almost buried up to the hilt. It entered in her midsection but had an upward thrust. The back door was banging in the wind.

* * *

"W I N S...W I N S...For music, news, time and the weather, keep your dial where the tens come together. W I N S 1010 on your radio dial, New York...bong...It's five o'clock...and now the news...The owner of a New Jersey delicatessen was found murdered this afternoon. Patrick Ganley arrived back at the store after running an errand to find the body of his wife, Susan Ganley. Mrs. Ganley had been stabbed to death..."

Tony Donohoo swung a U-turn to make a bee-line for Bergenfield and Ganley's Delicatessen.

He arrived at 5:15 P.M. to see Washington Avenue blocked off. At least half a dozen police vehicles could be seen with their red lights flashing. Tony parked three blocks away from the deli and walked. Several cops were trying to shepherd passersby along.

"There's nothing more to see here. Move along now....please keep moving."

Tony caught the attention of one cop and presented his I.D. and a business card. "Who's in charge?" he asked the cop.

"Detective Al McGuirl."

"Could you give him my card and tell him I'd like to have a word?" The cop nodded and disappeared through the front door of the deli, retuning in a few minutes, shaking his head.

"He says for you to take off. He has no time for you and you cannot come in the store. Sorry."

Tony nodded and walked back to the first cross street with a plan to approach the store from the back entrance, but two other cops were acting as sentries at the back door of the deli. Tony approached them and showed his I.D.

"What's the score, officer?" Tony asked.

"The broad that owns the joint was found with a kitchen knife sticking out of her. That's all we know."

"Is her husband in there?"

"Yeah, I think so."

"Can you give him this card and ask him to come out?"

"Yeah, okay," said the cop, and went through the door.

A few moments later, McGuirl burst through the door, red-faced and angry. "You didn't get the message, Donohoo? I said to shove off. This is no place for you. Now, get lost!"

"Let me talk to Ganley for a minute. What could it hurt?"

"The guy's wife has just been murdered. Ain't you got no respect?" Not waiting for an answer, McGuirl re-entered the store. Both cops were grinning.

Tony retraced his steps back to the car and headed for the office. He had calls to make.

Back at the office, Tony put in calls to the five living former jurors.

Malina Bankowski was not at her daughter's house in Pennsylvania, but he called her in Englewood to give her the news that the score was now seven jurors dead, five still breathing. He urged her once again not to be alone and to get out of town.

He called Andy Panzavecchia at O'Neill's Bar and Grill and was told that Andy was away on vacation. Maybe Andy was smarter that he looked.

He got Carol McKelvey at home and delivered the bad news, and repeated his warning.

Ed Gleason received the news with alarm. He indicated that he and his young wife were, indeed, getting out of Bergen County and would contact Tony in a day or two of how to reach him.

Liz Collins indicated that she had spoken to her employer, the owner of the Milestone Restaurant, who had sympathized with her dilemma and offered to put up Liz and her daughter in the owner's home in Englewood Cliffs. Liz had already taken up temporary residence the previous night, before even hearing about the murder of Susan Ganley. She gave Tony the phone number to reach her.

Mindy walked into the office during his conversation with Liz Collins. "What's going on?"

she asked.

"I'm glad you came. Susan Ganley has been murdered in her deli over in Bergenfield. Somebody stuck a big knife in her."

"Weren't you going there today?"

"I did go there. It was arranged that she would come here tonight. It was just before lunch and she was too busy to discuss anything with me. Now she can't discuss a goddamned thing."

"You want me to do anything?" Mindy asked.

"Yeah. I'd like you to go over to Haines' house in Maywood. Tell them what's happened. They'll know about it, of course, but see how they react."

"When did this happen?"

"McGuirl had me run off the scene without getting any information. One of the cops on the door said she had a kitchen knife stuck in her. I heard the report on the five o'clock news. The radio report said the husband left the store on an errand and found the body when he returned. I can't say when. Sometime this afternoon."

"I'll go now. I won't be seeing you tonight. Remember, I'll be at my sister's."

"If you have time, leave notes of your meeting with Haines on my desk before you go."

Tony's last call was to Brendan Cavanagh. He related the events of the afternoon.

"So what now? Do you have a list of suspects?"

"Well, there's the five living jurors. There's the defense attorney and his wife, who has turned up rather suspiciously in this case. I didn't buy the supposed attack on his life. It could be an attempt to exclude him as a suspect, but I think it was nothing more than a public relations attention grab. His practice is in the shithouse and could use a shot in the arm. Outside possibilities are Notella, the prosecuting attorney, and Judge Willcox. But I only include them because they could have known the identities of the jurors.

"And then, there are the surviving spouses of the seven victims - make that six - I'll exclude you," said Tony

"Thank you for that. But why any of the spouses?"

"If somebody wanted to get rid of their husband or wife, he or she would be the prime suspect. So they kill off a bunch of others that have something in common. In this case former jurors of a trial that went wrong. The motive then appears to a killer avenging Cassetti, but all but one of the murders are window dressing for the real intended victim."

"So why am I excluded?"

"You're the one who raised the issue. The killer would have left well enough alone. But I don't think it was one of the spouses. Four or five killings would be enough to mask the real motive and we're up to seven."

"Okay, thanks for calling. By the way, do you need any more money?"

"Yeah, thanks for asking. I was just getting around to that. I could use $500."

"It's in the mail."

* * *

Mindy rolled up in front of the Haines house and went to the door. Bob Haines answered the door bell, smiled and held the door open for Mindy. Thais was clearing away dinner dishes.

"I got bad news," Mindy led off. "Someone has murdered another one of the Cassetti jurors. Her name was Susan Ganley. She and her husband ran a deli in Bergenfield. Apparently her husband found the body in the store."

"Oh my God," said Bob Haines.

"That's seven of them," added Thais, shaking her head.

"Yeah, she got it this afternoon some time. I don't know yet just when. But Tony sent me because he felt you were entitled to be forewarned."

"Well, maybe Donohoo has a heart somewhere in there after all," said Bob, with a hint of a smile.

"He rubs me the wrong way," said Thais, returning from the kitchen, "but I gotta admit he's been on the money from the beginning."

"So what's your take on it, now?" Mindy asked to no one in particular.

"It surprises me that no one has made an attempt on Judge Willcox," said Bob. "After all, he's the one that gave the death penalty. Even accepting the jury's findings, he could have given Cassetti twenty or thirty years, or life in prison. of course, I'm not advocating the killer taking revenge against the judge, it just seems to follow."

"You know what surprises me?" said Mindy. "It's been at least several hours and no one has called to warn you. I would have expected Notella's office to notify you right off."

TWENTY-EIGHT

Tony busied himself developing Donald Jr.'s prints. He hung each picture from an eye-level wire with a clothes pin. He gave them just a quick glance, waiting to examine them carefully when they were dry. Mindy was babysitting two little nephews for her older sister, so he would be eating alone.

He went downstairs to the office and noticed Mindy's report on her meeting with Thais and Bob Haines. She made a point that the meeting had been one without rancor. Tony then went through the bookcase door.

After a couple of Old Grand Dads on the rocks and small talk with the patrons of the Yellow Front Saloon, he ordered the night's special, Hungarian Goulash over egg noodles. Tony ate his meal, as was his custom, with his back to the wall and a bottle of Schlitz. So when the last person he expected to see walked in, Tony saw him before he spotted Tony.

Tony threw up a hand to catch his eye, and having done so, motioned him back to the table.

"Your office is locked up. You said you'd be there at seven." Ganley was wearing the same clothes minus the apron.

"Mr. Ganley, I am deeply sorry for what's happened. I don't know what you must be feeling."

"I don't know yet myself. It hasn't hit me yet, I guess. But I can tell you one thing that's banging' around my head: I'm the biggest asshole that ever came down the pike."

"I came back to your store when I heard about it on the radio, but the cops wouldn't let me in."

"Yeah, one of the guys in uniform told me you was there, but that was later. I woulda come out if I knew. That big, fat ass cop, McGuirl—he don't know shit. When you came this morning, I figured you was like that Peter kid in the fairy tales crying wolf all the time. We had gotten a phone call from somebody in the prosecutor's office to watch out but it was no big deal, if you get me. So when you came in today, I thought if it was such a big deal we woulda heard more from the cops, but we didn't. So I heard what you said, but didn't take it to heart. I gotta live with that." His face twisted up and tears spilled out.

"How about a drink? I think you could use one." Ganley nodded and Tony signaled Sheena., the waitress.

"Gimme a Four Roses, no rocks and a beer chaser." Tony lip-synced "my tab" and told her to back Ganley up with another one, while having another Old Grand Dad for himself.

"You got kids?" Tony asked.

"Yeah, a boy in the Navy and a girl away at college. They're comin' in, but there's no hurry because the county's gonna do an autopsy, so the body can't be released for days."

"Are you up to telling me what happened?"

"Yeah, that's why I came." He threw down the shot of booze and took a sip of the beer.

"I left to go to the bank to make a deposit. It was about ten to three. Bank closes at three, but it's just down the street—half a block. I couldn't've been more than three or four minutes at the bank and I stopped at the newspaper store across from my deli to get cigarettes—maybe a couple more minutes. I was gone maybe ten minutes tops."

"Did you see anybody enter or leave the deli when you were on the way to the bank or on the way back?"

"No."

"What about when you were buying cigarettes?"

"No, nobody. When I walked into the store there was a lady at the counter. She sounded pissed off and asked if she could get service. There's a little bell that rings when the front door opens, so I asked her if my wife came out. She said no. She gave me her order, and I filled it and rang up her money."

"So she knew you worked there when you walked through the door?" Tony asked, pulling a Lucky out of the pack with his lips. He offered one to Ganley who put a stop sign up with his hand and took his own brand out. Tony snapped his Zippo open and lit them both.

"What do you mean?"

"Well, you walked in. Were you wearing an apron or anything?"

"No, I took it off before I left for the bank."

"But when you walked in, she asked for service. Why didn't she think you were another customer?"

"Well, I guess she saw me other times behind the counter."

"Is she a regular?"

"I don't remember ever seeing her before."

"You know my brother owns this saloon?"

"No, I didn't. So what?"

"Well, a lot of times he can't remember somebody's name but he knows what the guy's favorite drink is. He's talking to another bartender and says this guy was in last night and was three sheets to the wind. 'What's his name,' asked the other guy. "I don't know,' says my brother. 'You must know the guy: Apple Jack and Seven-Up.'"

"Why are you tellin' me this?" Ganley's expression was one of total confusion.

"What did the lady order?"

"Er...Kielbasi and Swiss cheese."

"Does that ring a bell?

"Oh, I see where you're going. But no, it don't mean nothing to me."

"Did the cops ask you about this lady?" Tony asked

"Not much. They asked me who she was and I said I didn't know. McGuirl said he was gonna put out an appeal for the woman to come forth."

"Describe her."

"She was tall, maybe 35. Brown hair. Nothing much to look at. Get lost in a crowd of two."

"What else? How was she dressed?"

"You think maybe she saw somethin'?"

"How do I know? I wasn't there. I'm asking you. How was she dressed?"

"She had on a coat. I guess she wore a dress under it."

"Close your eyes and picture her."

"Okay." Ganley shut his eyes. "Yeah, I can see her."

"What do you see?"

"She's got her purse in one hand on the counter but she never let go of it. Her dress had flowers on it. It hung lower than the coat. That's about it."

"When she left, did you see her go to a car?"

"No, as soon as she left, I went in the back and found Susan. I didn't give the lady a second thought."

"How did she pay you?"

"With a tenspot."

"And then you closed up the store?"

"Yeah, whatdya think? My wife was dead, for crissakes."

"What did you do with the money in the cash register?"

"I did what I always did. I put it in a strongbox to take home with me. I don't leave cash lying around the store overnight."

Tony gave the high sign to Sheena and made an index finger down stirring motion meaning another round of drinks. "Okay. When you go home, put on a pair of gloves. That tenner ought to be on top of the bills, right?"

"Well....yeah, it would be."

"Without touching it - you already did, of course - but don't touch it anymore. Put it in an envelope and take it to fat ass McGuirl and tell him about it. They may be able to raise the lady's fingerprints. Tell McGuirl it's your own idea. If he knows I told you, he won't do it."

"You think this lady is that important?"

"Hell, I don't know. I'm touching bases. We know she was there at the time of the murder or within a couple of minutes of it. So it would be negligent not to try to find her and ask what she saw or heard. She may even be the killer."

"You think they'd have her prints?"

"Probably not, unless she's been arrested for something or been in the Army. But if we find somebody later that looks good for the crime, we might get her prints and compare them. Sit tight for a couple of minutes. I gotta go next door to my office to get something. I'll be right back."

Tony returned with the photographs of the jurors and spread them out on the table. "Take a look at these and tell me if you've ever seen any of these people."

Ganley studied the pictures for a few minutes and finally shook his head.

"Okay, let's move onto something else. Think back to when Susan was on that jury. She was sequestered overnight, but when she came home, what did she tell you about it?"

"She disliked that Cassetti guy. She said he was a real bastard. He beat up his wife and kids all the time."

"There were a number of jurors who were for conviction the first day,"Tony said, "but there were a few holdouts. From what I could gather, it wasn't so much that they thought he was not guilty as they just didn't want to make a decision. It was those few that caused the jury to be held overnight. Now where was Susan on this issue?"

"She was for conviction the first day. I remember her being critical of the ones that weren't. She said the evidence was staring them right in the face."

"Did McGuirl ask you about that?"

"How she voted on the jury? No. It didn't come up."

"Was Susan remorseful when it turned out that Cassetti was not the guy after all? How did she feel about that?"

"She said he was still a first class sonovabitch and it was his own goddamned fault. She sympathized more with that mob guy who actually did it because he wasn't there to kill the lady but to burglarize the house and she pulled a gun on him. The gun went off while he was taking it away from her. It woulda just been manslaughter or maybe even self-defense if it didn't happen during the commission of a crime. Oh, yeah, she thought Cassetti was a prick of the first order." Ganley had thrown down the third drink and his words were slurring a little. In his emotional state, the booze seemed to get into the bloodstream and brain in half the time.

Tony was beginning to feel the effects as well.

"When I came into the store this morning, I could tell you didn't like me. And yet, here you are.

Why have you come to me?"

"When I was a little kid, there was a grouchy old maid on my street named Miss Applegate. We called her Miss Crabapple. She didn't like kids and was always yelling at us to stay off her grass and stop making so much noise. That sort of thing. When I was about eight years old, we was playing ball in front of her house, and the ball went up on the lawn. I went to get it, but she came off the porch and got it first and told me to get out of her yard. I got mad and threw a stone at her. It missed but she said she was callin' the cops and that I was goin' to jail. I was scared shit. I ran home and confessed the whole thing to my mother, cryin' my eyes out.

"My mother told me to dry my eyes. She made me promise not to throw stones at people again. Then she'd have a talk with Miss Applegate and don't worry because the police didn't put little boys in jail. And I felt fine because my mother was taking care of everything. You Catholic?"

"Yeah, why?" answered Tony.

"Because it's kinda like goin' to confession, you know. You dump your sins into the priest's lap, and they become his problem. I came to you because you're the one that got it right. I was wrong but my mother's too old to handle this, so I come to you. I feel better for doin' so. Now let me buy you a drink."

TWENTY-NINE

Saturday, October 24, 1953, 10:00 A.M.

Tony sauntered into the office with a small bag of doughnuts from the Main Street Bakery. Mindy had already put on a pot of coffee. She selected a plain cruller and Tony picked out a Boston cream-filled doughnut. As they sipped coffee, Tony described his meeting with Patrick Ganley the previous night. Mindy smiled and chuckled that Ganley saw Tony as some sort of priestly confessor.

She had stacked up the funeral parlor sign-in books from six different wakes: Cavanagh, Geiger, Jackson, Jenkins, Nagle and Recchion.

"Did you ever notice that when people die young there's a lot more people at the funerals? I got into the guest registers from the funeral homes," Mindy said. "It's slow going. Every book has at least eight or ten people that the family didn't know. I had to take each such name and compare it to all the other unknown guests in the other five books. So far, I got nothing. I'm about halfway through."

Tony stood and went to the blackboard and wrote the names of the twelve jurors, indicating next to each name D for dead or L for living and how they voted at the end of the first day of jury deliberation. G for guilty and NG for not guilty, according to the statements of the living jurors, and the next of kin of the dead ones: "There does not seem to be any motive for any of these people to lie about how the vote went. If we later run into a road block, we can go back and reconsider it." Mindy took another bite out of her cruller and sipped her coffee.

"Okay, I'll buy that," said Tony.

> Marcy Cavanagh D G
> Liz Collins L NG
> Susan Ganley D G
> Kathleen Geiger D G
> Ed Gleason L NG
> Norman Jackson D G
> Charlie Jenkins D G
> Malina Bankowski L NG
> Carol McKelvey L NG
> Donald Nagle D G
> Andy Panda L NG
> Theresa Froumy D G

"So that shows that all of those who were ready to convict on the first day have been killed," Mindy said.

"And conversely," Tony added, "all those not ready to vote for conviction on the first day are still walking around. The original suspect list contained 27 people including Andy Panda, eight jurors that were then unknown, both Cassetti sons, possibly twelve spouses of jurors, Judge Willcox, Prosecutor Notella, defense attorney Haines, and the erstwhile Ezekiel Fussbucket. Then we added Patricia Zipoli and Thais Haines, which made 29 suspects."

"Now," continued Tony, "we're left with five jurors, Liz Collins, Ed Gleason, Malina Bankowski, Carol McKelvey, and Andy Panda. I think we can rule out the fishnet killer theory. Four or five murders would have more than sufficed to focus the attention away from a single intended victim with the others being window dressing. A letter from Harry Cassetti Jr.'s commanding officer states that he's been in Korea since January with a couple of R&R's into Tokyo. There's no way he could come back to Jersey every month to kill somebody. He's out of it. The brother Stephen makes no sense either, and I'm willing to scratch him."

"We threw in Thais Haines and Patricia Zipoli, but I think they have to be removed from the list also," said Mindy.

"Why?"

"Because the pattern is that the victims are all people that didn't want to give Harry Cassetti the benefit of the doubt. How could anyone else know that who wasn't in the jury room?"

"By that thinking, and I'm not saying I disagree, that would also remove Judge Willcox, Lou Notella and Bob Haines, unless you give them credit for being able to read people with total accuracy."

"So we're down to the five living jurors," Mindy said.

"And Ezekiel Fussbucket."

"Ezekiel looks more and more unlikely."

"We can't get ahead of ourselves," said Tony. "Who says the killings are over?"

THIRTY

Mindy got back to work on the funeral registers. Tony studied the photographs taken by Donald Nagle Jr. of his father's wake, funeral and luncheon. Nothing turned up in either endeavor. There was no one in any of the photographs that Tony recognized except for Christine Nagle, who looked good in black.

Tony had a lunch date with Brendan Cavanagh at Holly's Restaurant on Route 4 at noon. Tony arrived at five minutes before the hour to find Cavanagh at a table waiting for him..

They ordered sandwiches and coffee and Cavanagh got right to it.

"So where are we?"

"I saw Patrick Ganley last night. He says that his wife was adamant about convicting Cassetti. That means that of the seven jurors who are dead, all of them wanted to convict on the first day of deliberation. The five living jurors all voted not guilty the first day."

"So that tells you there's an avenging angel—or devil—at work? How does that narrow the field of suspects?"

"Who would know that? Who, besides the twelve people

in the jury room would know, by name, who voted which way?"

"So you're saying it's one of the five living jurors. Who are they again?"

"There's two men. Ed Gleason and Andy Panzavecchia. Three women. Carol McKelvey, Liz Collins and Malina Bankowski. I pretty much have to rule out Liz Collins, because she's barely five feet tall and about 100 pounds. I can't see her hoisting Kathleen Geiger up to hang her by the neck."

"Or overpowering Marcy out by the swimming float," added Brendan. "So what's your next move?"

"I'm thinking about doing something unorthodox, but I wanted your permission to do it first."

"What's that?"

"Typing up my notes on this case and giving them to Detective Al McGuirl. Just for example, I would have difficulty going to the living jurors and asking them for alibis yesterday afternoon, but McGuirl could do it. Also he was in control of the crime scenes of Jenkins and Ganley. He may have seen something I don't know about. Look, I can't stand the sight of his fat ass. He's bad-tempered, arrogant, closed-minded and none too bright, but the objective is to find the killer."

"Well, don't you think he's checked their alibis?"

"I doubt if he has narrowed it down to the five living jurors. In his investigation, I don't think he focused on how the different victims voted."

"So, you're asking me for permission to turn over your

notes? Do you need my permission?"

"You're paying for the investigation. How would you feel if he gets my notes, cracks the case and takes all the credit. Do I still get paid?"

"Put that thought out of your mind. You've come a long way in just two weeks. McGuirl will have to be grateful for the help, I'm sure."

"You're only sure because you don't know the fat bastard. He may not even read the notes, but if he does and it helps him, you won't see my name in the paper when it's over. He'll take all the credit, which is fine with me as far as everyone but you is concerned. I expect you to credit me and write a check."

"Don't worry about it. You have my full support."

"Good. I'll give him the notes."

"Stay in touch," said Cavanagh.

* * *

Tony arrived back at the office and began to type the notes taken by himself and Mindy. He prepared them with an original and two carbons. The transcribed notes were more or less complete. He skipped over his process for getting license plates identified. He deliberated whether or not to tell McGuirl about Patricia Zipoli being Cassetti's sister. In the end, he omitted it. He also left out that Carol McKelvey had kept a pistol in her hand during the entire interview. His version was in true report style with facts being stated, or most of them, but not hunches, opinions or theories, which all would be lost on McGuirl anyway. Each comment listed its source. Having completed the notes, Tony conferred with Mindy about her reports for accuracy. He stuffed them into a manila envelope and drove over to County Police Headquarters to hand-deliver them.

"I'd like to see Detective McGuirl," Tony said to the officer on the desk. "I'm Tony Donohoo."

McGuirl surfaced from the bowels of the police station with a look of disgust on his face. "If you've come to get information on the jury case, you can take a U-turn right now," said McGuirl, without inviting Tony to meet with him in an interview room.

"I haven't come to get information but to give you what I've got. Don't forget I was on this case before you." Tony handed him the envelope which had some weight to it.

"So you're saying I should read all this crap? Like I got nothin' better to do?"

"Wipe your fat ass with it for all I care. But remember I gave it to you." The cop on the desk tried, without success, to suppress a laugh. Tony walked out shaking his head.

* * *

Mindy in green with her shoulder length red hair, was an eye-catching sight to behold. When Tony and Mindy entered the famous 1776 House in Tappan, New York, many heads in the dining room turned to the handsome couple. The 1776 House had operated continuously as a tavern since the American Revolution and had been used to try Major

John Andre for treason. Andre, an American officer, was found guilty of spying for the British and hung from a nearby oak tree. While modern concessions had been incorporated, such as indoor restrooms, by and large it was authentic 18th century. Next door was a smaller building that had been used as George Washington's headquarters. Located just a few hundred yards from the northernmost New Jersey border, its patronage was split down the middle between New York and New Jersey residents. The specialties of the house were steaks and chops.

After ordering a pair of dry martinis - olive for Tony, lemon peel for Mindy - they both settled on lamb chops. Waitresses in semi-18th century outfits including pinafores and mob caps, provided service.

After dinner, Tony and Mindy relaxed with coffee, cigarettes and a liqueur, enjoying a respite from dead jurors, Big Al McGuirl, Bob and Thais Haines, and a host of others.

They arrived at the Park Lane Theater in Palisade Park with five minutes to spare for the nine o'clock showing of *The Quiet Man* filmed entirely in Ireland, and starring John Wayne, Maureen O'Hara and Victor McLaglen, which was not the first time that trio had shared the silver screen. Director John Ford peppered the cast with a number of his favorites including brothers Barry Fitzgerald and Arthur Shields, Mildred Natwick and Ward Bond.

On the drive back to Tony's apartment, Mindy observed:"That fight scene went on forever, It must have lasted a half-hour. Is that realistic?"

"Hell, no," said Tony. "Nobody could fight that long,

and they must have covered nearly a mile from beginning to end. But there's a great story about the movie. It was filmed in the Village of Cong in County Mayo," said Tony. "just a few miles from Galway. They had no electric power there and the movie company had to bring it in at considerable expense. When the shooting was done and the company was packing up to leave, John Ford went to the mayor of the village and offered to leave all the cables, transformers and utility poles in place, as a gift to the people of Cong. 'But, of course,' said Ford, 'from now on, the townspeople will have to pay for what power they use.'

"Ford was bowled over a couple of days later when the mayor reported back that he had polled the villagers and they said 'take it all with you when you go.'"

THIRTY-ONE

Monday, October 26, 1953, 10:00 A. M.

Tony slept in that morning. When he came down to the office, Alice had left two telephone messages on his desk. One was from a divorce lawyer who was good for three or four referrals each year. The other from the Peoples State Bank in Paramus, which was also a repeat source of business.

He called the lawyer first.

The lawyer had a divorce client who had figured out his wife was having an affair. As in most cases of this type, the husband had already done some of his own detective work, and knew when his wife would habitually meet with her boyfriend and even who the guy was.

What he needed from Tony was to catch her in the act, photograph her and the boyfriend coming out of a motel, and testify in court to what he observed. A payday for Tony. He decided that the dead juror mystery could be put on the back burner for a couple of days. After all, he had provided the cops with his notes and Tony now believed there would be no further killings, with the possible exception of Patrick

Ganley.

The lawyer went on to say the client was with him in the office and could he send the guy over to handle the details and answer Tony's questions. Tony agreed and was told the client, one Peter Rossi, would be there in twenty minutes.

He called the bank and asked for the loan officer, Ronald St. Lawrence. St. Lawrence got on and said the bank had made a loan of $4,000 for the purchase of a new Cadillac four months earlier. The borrower, one Eustace Renahan, had made not one single payment. A brief investigation by the loan officer revealed Renahan's phone number was disconnected and that he no longer lived at the same address. His employer, Patriot Building Alternatives, Inc., where he had been a salesman, indicated he was no longer employed. The bank wanted to repossess the car but had no idea where Renahan had gone. St. Lawrence added that if and when Tony located Mr. Renahan, that he was providing the necessary paperwork for Tony to repossess the car.

Tony took notes and told St. Lawrence he would get back to him later in the day.

As he finished with the call, Alice buzzed him there was a Mr. Rossi waiting to see him.

"Send him in, please."

Peter Rossi entered the office, and Tony rose to shake his hand. He was about forty, and dressed in a brown pin-striped suit.

"I understand that you're seeking a divorce on the grounds of infidelity, but that your wife is not yet aware of that. Is that correct?"

"Yes, she doesn't know that I know she's sleeping with another guy, and my lawyer wants me to keep it that way until we get the goods on her," Rossi said.

"How did you find out?"

"It was a fluke. You know a motel on Route 46 called the "Fly-Inn" just across the highway from Teterboro Airport?"

"Yeah, I know the place," Tony answered. The real estate agency, F. X. Donohoo, Realtors, which shared office space, receptionist, telephones and research materials with Tony's detective agency, was owned by Frankie, his wife, Dolly, and Tony in three equal parts. Both Frankie and Tony held broker licenses, but Dolly ran the show. Dolly didn't like to deal with commercial real estate and when the opportunity arose in 1952 to list the "Fly-Inn Motel," she asked Tony to deal with the owner.

In doing so, one of Tony's questions to the owner was:"What's your occupancy rate?" If there were forty rooms and twenty were rented on average each night, the rate would be fifty percent.

"150%," came the answer.

"150%? You can't have an average of 150%. 100% is as high as you can go." said Tony.

"Bullshit! I rent out at least half these rooms twice every night."

So Tony was familiar with the "Fly-Inn Motel."

"There's a car wash right next door to the motel," continued Rossi. "It only has about fifty feet frontage on Route 46, and there's only room for this long driveway, and then you make a left turn and the actual car wash is behind the motel.

Most of the parking lot is behind the motel. So about a month ago, I'm going through the car wash. As I get out of the car, I look over the fence and there's my wife's car parked behind the motel. There's a lounge at the car wash where you can wait if you're getting a wax job or something, so I just sat back and hung out. Half an hour later out she comes with this guy. They talk for a couple of minutes standing next to her car, then they kiss and she gets in the car and leaves."

"Was her car parked near the room?"

"Yeah, like most motels, you park right in front of the door to the room."

"Your lawyer said you knew who the guy was."

"Yeah, his name is Wayne Koller. I met him at my wife's twenty year high school reunion just a few months ago. He danced with her twice. I understand they were an item in high school. and it looks like the flame has been relit."

"What's your wife's name?"

"Charlotte."

"You got a picture?"

Rossi pulled one out of his pocket.

"Hm-m, pretty," said Tony. "Let me have height, weight, that sort of thing."

"She's about five-six, maybe one-thirty. Good figure."

"And she's what? Late thirties?"

"Yeah, thirty-eight last month."

"What day of the week was this at the motel? And what time of day?"

"Wednesday. Around eleven in the morning. For the last

few weeks, I've called the house about eleven several times and she's always there except on Wednesdays."

"You got kids?"

"Two. The girl is the older. She's ten. The boy is eight."

"Your wife doesn't work?"

"Nah, she talks about going back to work after the youngest is old enough to carry a latch key, but that won't be for another three years or so."

"What do you do, Mr. Rossi?"

"I'm a salesman. I sell paint, mostly to hardware stores. My territory is Bergen, Passaic and Morris Counties, and Rockland County in New York State."

"Your wife has her own car, you said. What is it?"

"1950 gray Chevy four-door."

"You know the plate number?"

"BRO 21 F."

"Okay, this is my service agreement. The retainer is $300 non-refundable. I get $35 per day plus expenses. Unless she's changed her M.O., I probably won't have to come back to you for more money.

For that, I will get photographs of them coming out of the motel, and hopefully some kind of inclination, which is a requirement in New Jersey for a divorce. It's not enough for two people to just be in a car together."

"Whadya mean, inclination?"

"Hugging, kissing, that sort of thing."

"When do you start?"

"We'll be on her Wednesday morning, if she cooperates. Put your address down on the agreement and I'll need your approval at the bottom, and, of course, your check."

* * *

Tony arrived at Peoples State Bank just a couple of minutes short of noon and caught St. Lawrence as he was leaving for lunch. He gave Tony the paperwork for the repo.

"I still get $35 per day, but I've raised the price of repossessing the car from $40 to $50."

"Aw, how come?" asked St. Clair.

"Because it's dangerous, that's how come."

"Come on, have you ever been hurt picking up a car?"

"When I find the guy, I'll just tell you where the car is and you can go get it. Then you can tell your boss how you saved the fifty and how safe it was."

"All right, you get the fifty," conceded St. Lawrence.

The bank's information sheet gave the former home address and the former employer's address in Fort Lee. Tony opted for the employer first. He arrived at the Fort Lee address to find a hand-written note on the door saying "We've moved effective September 1st. We're now located at 318 Palisade Avenue, Cliffside Park."

Tony stopped at Callahan's Hot Dog Stand in Fort Lee for a foot-long with sauerkraut and a short beer. By one o'clock he was at the new address in a shabby three-story office building. No elevator and Patriot Building Alternatives, Inc. was on the second floor. Samples on a coffee table in a tiny waiting area showed their product was aluminum siding. A business license in a cheap frame hung on the wall.

A man came out in a short sleeve plaid shirt and stared at Tony for a few seconds. It was obvious that visitors to the office were not common.

"Can I help you?"

"Yes, Good afternoon. I'm Tony Donohoo, New Jersey State Detective." He presented his shield. "I'd like to speak to Eustace Renahan, please."

"He don't work here no more."

"Well, he witnessed an auto accident last year and it's going to court next week. I need to speak to him. Can you give me his forwarding address, please, along with his phone number?"

"No, we ain't got that information."

"May I see his personnel file, please?"

"You got a warrant?"

"No. Do I need one?"

"You do if you want to see his personnel file."

"You know it's a pleasure to run into someone who does things by the book. I like to do things by the book also. For example, when a business concern changes location, the county license registrar is to be notified within seven days. and a new business license is issued for the new address. Failure to comply will render all contracts or sales entered into after the seven days invalid and all moneys received to be returned to the customers. Oh, gosh," continued Tony, walking over to the business license hanging on the wall. "This has the Fort Lee address on it. and you moved here on September first, almost two months ago. Well, I'm sure that's just an oversight on your part. Maybe the county will give you a break."

"I'll get you the file," said the man.

The file revealed that Eustace was not formerly employed but was now the branch manager for a newly opened office of Patriot Building Alternatives, Inc. in Jersey City.

Tony copied the information down including his new residence and the address of the new office.

"Now, if I get even the hint that you called Renahan and warned him that I'm coming to see him," said Tony, changing his tone, "then I'll be back and you'll be in deep, deep shit. Do you read me?"

"Yeah, I got it." What, of course, the manager did not know was that the penalty for failure to notify the authority for a change of business address license called for a fine of $25, which could be waived for a first offense, and had no bearing on the obligations of the parties to any contract.

* * *

By two-thirty, Tony was back at the office. Mindy was doing paperwork.

"Let's go," he said. "You gotta drive me down to Jersey City for a car repossession. I want to get it out of the way today." Tony went into his desk and brought out a large key ring with about twenty keys on it, all for General Motors automobiles. One of those keys would surely start Renahan's Cadillac. There was also a Chrysler product key ring, one for the Ford Motor Company, and a miscellaneous ring which had keys for Kaisers, Packards or Willys.

Tony spotted the crystal green Coupe De Ville parked curbside on Communipaw Avenue in Jersey City. Mindy dropped him off and within two minutes, he had started the car and inched it into the traffic flow. As he crept along, a man, who he guessed was Eustace Renahan, rushed out of a building screaming obscenities and ran alongside the Caddie trying to open the passenger side door, which Tony had had the foresight to lock. Finally traffic opened up and that was the last that Eustace Renahan was ever to see of his crystal green Coupe De Ville.

THIRTY -TWO

Wednesday, October 28, 1953, 9:00 A. M. Bogota, New Jersey.

The Rossi house was on Beechwood Avenue, a residential street about a quarter mile long which t-boned into two other busier thoroughfares. Mindy sat near the intersection at one end of Beechwood Avenue and Tony was parked near the other. They had walkie-talkies for this type of surveillance.

At about 9:55, Mindy's voice sounded: "She's on the move. I've got her going south on Queen Anne Road. Grey Chevy, BRO 21 F."

"Stay with her. I'll parallel you for a few blocks and then cut over."

"I got her. No problem."

Tony picked up speed to take his position in view of the pursuit.

"We're at a traffic light in Ridgefield Park. She's two cars ahead of me in the line," Mindy transmitted.

"All right, I'm just a couple of blocks back. When I give you the word, turn that Kelly green eyesore off to the right and I'll move into your position." If Charlotte Rossi had been noticing the Kelly green Ford convertible, she would be mollified when it turned off.

"Okay, I'm in place," Tony said.

Mindy took the next right into a side street and then did a u-turn to come back onto Queen Anne Road a block or two behind Tony.

When Charlotte Rossi reached Route 46, she proceeded west, and Mindy and Tony followed in their separate vehicles. Several miles further, Mrs. Rossi turned into the parking lot of the "Fly-Inn Motel" as expected. They watched her drive around the building to park in the rear of the building out of sight to anyone on the highway. Mindy and Tony both pulled into the parking lot of the Bendix Diner and went in for coffee. They would wait for about fifteen minutes to be sure that the boyfriend had time to arrive and they both settled into the room. The rooms at the rear of the building had doors that faced the rear parking lot.

Tony and Mindy shared a Danish. Then, leaving Mindy's more conspicuous car at the diner, drove into the Fly-Inn Motel parking lot, taking down the license plate number of every car in the lot whether in the front or rear.

They took up a position in the rear parking lot that offered an excellent view of Charlotte's gray Chevrolet. She probably knew what room her boyfriend had reserved in advance and parked near it. It was 10:35 by the time Tony selected a parking space. Charlotte had already been in the room a full twenty minutes. They waited with cameras ready.

At 11:20, Charlotte and a tall man with dark hair came out of the room. Tony and Mindy clicked away with their respective cameras. After a brief verbal exchange, Charlotte stood on tiptoe and kissed the man on the lips. Inclination in spades! And both Tony and Mindy had caught it on film.

THIRTY-THREE

Thursday, October 29, 1953, 7:30 P.M.

For the second time in two weeks, Tony and Mindy found themselves at the Timothy P. Kelly Home for Funerals in Dumont, for the Ganley funeral. Mindy wore loose flowing clothes to cover her curvaceousness, and window pane horn rim spectacles. She attended the wake armed with a low-light camera that was concealed to look like a pack of Pall Mall cigarettes.

Meanwhile, Tony worked the parking lot taking down all the license plate numbers. Once again, he attracted the attention of a handful of smokers standing on the veranda, but was not approached.

There were a good many cars that clearly belonged to teenagers. Pre-war cars with foxtails attached to radio antennas, chrome removed, objects dangling from the rear-view mirrors, told the tale. Tony noticed the gear shift knob on an open convertible had an earlier life as the handle on the draft beer dispenser for Pabst Blue Ribbon Beer. Clearly, these cars belonged to youthful friends of the son and daughter of Susan Ganley.

Mindy emerged from the funeral parlor about eight-fifteen. She had several funeral cards with a picture of the Blessed Virgin on one side and the name of Susan Mary Ganley on the reverse with a prayer. Ten minutes later they had taken a booth at the Clinton Inn in Tenafly and ordered drinks.

"I stayed clear of everyone. I didn't get into the line to pay respects to the family. The husband stood there with his daughter one one side and his son on the other in his Navy blue bell-bottoms. There were a bunch of college-age kids there," Mindy reported. "plus four other sailors in uniform. It's called paying respect, but it's really curiosity. They're young and unaccustomed to death. They wear somber faces as cover. It's like when they sing along with love songs in the presence of someone they've got a crush on.. It enables them to say things they otherwise couldn't get the nerve up to say."

"Did you get a lot of shots?"

"I reloaded twice in the ladies' room. I think I got everybody who was there. There had to be a hundred or more. Catching bits and pieces of conversations, I could tell that many of them were delicatessen customers. Lonely people."

"What do you mean, 'lonely people?' People who go into delicatessens are lonely?"

"No, I don't mean that. Some people, who I think of as being lonely, often will make small talk with clerks, who are a captive audience," said Mindy. "It can be annoying because they can hold up a line talking about the weather or something, but I remind myself they're starved for conversation with another human being."

"That's what I like about you, Mindy. You come on as being no-nonsense and cynical, but you're actually kinda warm and cuddly."

"Shut up, Tony."

"Did you notice any cops? Tony asked.

"Yeah, there were two guys in plain clothes that I've seen before."

"Maybe McGuirl is actually waking up," said Tony.

THIRTY-FOUR

Friday, October 30, 1953, 4:45 P.M.

Mindy was off doing a photo shoot for the *Bergen Evening Record*. Tony had made arrangements with Pat Ganley to pick up the guest register from the funeral home with the unknowns checked off. Ganley had checked off over thirty of them. Doubtlessly, most of them were customers of the deli that Ganley would know by sight but not by name. He spent the morning working on developing Mindy's shots taken at the wake. He was unable to recognize anyone except Patrick Ganley. After a burger and a beer in the Yellow Front Saloon, he turned his attention to posting the license plate file. The cross-referencing of the yellow lined sheets took a lot of time. Again, nothing usable showed up.

"You got a call on line three," came Alice's voice on his intercom. Alice was expert in screening his calls or visitors. "You'll want to take it. It's Pete."

"Yeah, Pete. What's up?" Tony asked of his quasi-cousin.

"I just got a tele-type. This is gonna knock you right on your ass. A woman named Malina Bankowski has been found dead. In Englewood. Her home. Get this. She was found handcuffed to the bumper of her car in her garage. The motor was running and she was asphyxiated."

"Holy Christ! Who found her?"

"Her husband, when he got home from work. It mentions that she was one of the Cassetti jurors and she's the eighth one to take the stairway to heaven."

"McGuirl in charge?"

"Yeah, I'm guessing the prosecutor would recognize this is the same case and appoint him to handle the investigation," said Pete.

"I gave him my notes on the case last week."

"Did he thank you?"

"I think his exact words were 'Do you expect me to read this crap?' I told him I didn't care if he wiped his ass with them."

"Nice going. He really is a major league asshole. I'll let you know if I get anything else."

Tony hopped in his Ford and headed over to the Bankowski home. It was on the south end of town near the Leonia line. The house was a two-story frame house built in the 1920's. The garage was detached at the rear of the lot.

It would be a great time to rob a bank in Englewood because most of the police force was in evidence. Tony parked a couple of doors down and approached on foot. Several of the uniformed cops walked toward him as he approached to ward him off. Tony flashed his shield and asked if McGuirl was around.

"Yeah, he's in the house with the woman's husband."

"Tell him I'd like to talk with him. I'm Tony Donohoo."

The cop returned in a minute. "McGuirl will stop by your office tomorrow at 9:30. He also said that if you asked, you were not to be allowed on the scene."

"Yeah, well, I didn't ask," said Tony.

Tony decided it was the best time to canvas the immediate neighborhood to see if anybody saw anything. He knocked on each of the doors of the next door neighbors, showing his shield and credentials. In both cases, a women answered the door. He asked if they had been home all day and if they had seen Malina Bankowski or anybody else coming to visit. Neither one had seen anything to report. Next he tried the three houses across the street. Two were negative, but the lady in the house directly opposite mentioned having seen Malina around noon time.

"She pulled her car into the driveway and got out and she must have gone in by the back door, which is out of sight."

"You're sure it was her?" asked Tony.

"Oh, yeah. It was her car and she was wearing her green coat and a kerchief on her head. She often wears a kerchief."

* * *

7:00 P.M.

Tony and Mindy sat down at a table in the Yellow Front Saloon. That night's special was lasagna and both opted for it along with a house salad, a wedge of a quarter-head of iceberg lettuce, with sliced tomatoes, in a large wooden bowl and served with a stainless steel caddy with four dressings.

"We'll take a couple of beers, Sheena. Schlitz for me and a Pabst's for Mindy." Tony then related to Mindy what had occurred.

"Well, it sounds like murder," she said. "What do you think?"

"I don't know. McGuirl's coming to the office tomorrow at 9:30. He's never done that before.

He might want to talk about Mrs. Bankowski being the only victim out of eight who didn't want to convict Cassetti."

"Was there a suicide note?" Mindy asked.

"I don't know. I never heard of anyone handcuffing herself to a car in a closed garage with the motor running. That's one for the books."

"That does throw a wrench into our theory, doesn't it?"

"What the hell was she even doing in Englewood? I told her to get out of town and stay with her daughter in Pennsylvania."

"Oh my. And someone didn't do what you told them to do? How could that happen?"

* * *

Saturday morning, 9:15 A.M.

Tony stopped by the Main Street Bakery and picked up a half dozen doughnuts. He put a pot of coffee on. Since McGuirl was making an effort to communicate, Tony could meet him halfway. At 9:35 Alice buzzed him saying there was a *man* to see him. That was Alice-ese for someone she did not like on sight.

"Send him in," Tony responded into the intercom. A few moments later, McGuirl came through with a file folder under his arm.

"Coffee and doughnuts, Al?" Using McGuirl's first name almost made Tony gag, but he got it out.

"Yeah, don't mind if I do." Tony had guessed that McGuirl was a jelly doughnut guy and so had gotten several of them.

"Help yourself."

"So it looks like your theory just went down the terlet," said McGuirl.

"What theory is that?"

"Your theory that only the ones who voted to convict the first day get killed."

"I didn't give you any theory."

"I read your stuff. That's where you were going alright."

"I just reported the facts. Those aren't *my* facts, those are *the* facts. Let's get to it. Is it murder or suicide?"

"I got it as suicide. She handcuffed herself to the car with the motor running inside the garage."

"That's a first for me. Why would a someone committing suicide handcuff herself to a car?

"Probably just in case she got cold feet. Besides, the key to the cuffs was in her pocket. What kind of killer would leave the key in the pocket?"

"Suicide note?"

"Nope."

"Prints on the handcuffs?"

"Just hers."

"Why would she commit suicide?" Tony asked.

"How the hell would I know? Maybe she felt guilty or sumthin'"

"Did you canvas the neighborhood?"

"I got a couple of guys doing that right now."

"They get a read on how long she was dead?"

"The medical examiner said two to three hours, but he may be able to get closer when he does the autopsy," said McGuirl.

"Are you looking at the husband?"

"He says he got home about 3:15 and found her. Called it in right away. Says he was working and got off at three."

"Anybody check it out?"

"I got one of the guys doing that this morning. Bankowski works at a paper bag factory down in Ridgefield. Ten-fifteen minute drive." McGuirl had managed to get powdered sugar down his shirt front.

"I know you didn't come here to fill me in on what's happened," said Tony. "You must want to know something. Before we get to what you want, let me ask you a question."

"Yeah, what?"

"Ganley told me you were gonna put out some kind of appeal for the lady that was in the deli when Ganley returned from the bank. Did anything come of that?"

"Nah, not a thing."

"Okay, so let's move on to what you want," said Tony.

"Yeah. You went up to Sunrise Lake in New York State. Why'd you do that?"

"That's where Marcy Cavanagh drowned."

"Yeah, who'd you talk to there?" McGuirl helped himself to another jelly doughnut. His tie now had a big drop of strawberry jelly on it. Tony removed the one Boston cream and took a big bite.

"Well, there was the lady who owns an old fashioned lunch wagon...one of her customers. A guy who runs a boatyard—Smitty, he calls himself. There's a little general store with a post office counter and boxes. Didn't get much out of her...and the next door neighbors of the Cavanaghs. Zipoli is their name. In October it's like a ghost town up there."

"Tell me about the orange bathing cap."

"You did read my notes. Good." Tony popped out a couple of Luckies and offered one to McGuirl. Tony lit them both up with his Zippo.

"I ain't as dumb as I look. What about the orange bathing cap?"

"The boatyard guy—Smitty—said he saw someone with an orange bathing cap swimming off shore at his side of the lake. He said it was a woman, but when I asked him how he could be sure, he said he'd never seen a man wearing one of those caps. So what it came down to was that he just assumed it was a woman. She or he was about 100 yards out when he saw her or him. I asked him if the swimmer made it to the other side of the lake where the Cavanagh woman drowned - maybe a quarter mile - but he didn't notice. Why the interest in the orange bathing cap?"

"Because there was one in the trunk of Mrs. Bankowski's car. Did you talk to anybody about it?"

"I asked the Zipolis if Marcy Cavanagh wore one. They said she didn't wear any bathing cap."

"Where can I reach these people?"

"They live in Dumont."

"You got a street address?"

"Yeah, but I gotta tell you something if you're going over there. Mrs. Zipoli is the sister of Harry Cassetti."

"Jesus H. Christ, Donohoo! You've been holdin' out on me." McGuirl almost came out of his chair.

"You're right. I'm sorry. I promised the lady it wouldn't come from me unless it was necessary. She doesn't want it to be common knowledge that Cassetti was her brother."

"You sonovabitch. Holdin' out on me."

"Hey, up yours, McGuirl. Did I keep you from going up to Sunrise Lake? Did I slash your tires so you couldn't go to Bridgeport and interview Cassetti's son? So you sit on your fat ass here in Bergen County and then get pissed off when somebody else does actual detective work!"

"All right, all right. So you're tellin' me that this Cavanagh woman sat on a jury trying her next door neighbor's brother for murder?"

"That's what I'm telling you."

"And you don't think that's a motive for this Zipoli dame?"

"A motive to kill seven other people? No, I don't think it's a motive. Someone could argue that, but how would she have known which jurors voted which way?"

"So it *is* your theory that it's one of the jurors."

"Yeah, that's one theory I considered, but I didn't include that in my notes."

"So, how do you feel now that the most reluctant of them all got it? Kinda sinks your boat, don't it?"

"No, it doesn't, because I know who murdered Malina Bankowski," said Tony.

"WHAT? You've not only decided it's murder but you know who did it?"

"That's right. I can't prove it right now, but I know who did it."

"Well, who the hell is it?"

"Not now, Al, not now. You'll be in on the bust. But you've got my notes, which means, you've got what I've got."

THIRTY-FIVE

Thursday, November 5, 1953, 7:30 P. M. - Robert J. Paladino Home for Funerals, Englewood, New Jersey.

Once again, Mindy in her semi-disguise and her Pall Mall camera roamed a wake. This time, family and mourners of Malina Bankowski filled up the Paladino Funeral Home. The widower, Stanley Bankowski, stood in front of the closed casket flanked by three young adults - two women and a man. Mindy took them to be the children of the deceased. She got several shots of a table that contained framed photographs: a gap-toothed six year old in middie blouse and pigtails, a wedding portrait, a thirty year-old Malina with toddlers on the beach, A relatively recent shot of the husband and a kerchief-wearing Malina in front of the Lincoln Memorial, and as a smiling teen in a bathing suit with a medal around her neck. The pictured medal dangled from the top of the frame. The medal was a two-inch disc that read:

(Bas-relief of a girl swimming)
ST. CECILIA HIGH SCHOOL

(A long blue ribbon was threaded through a hole at the top of the medal to enable the recipient to wear it around the neck. Three small rectangular bars were attached below the medal with a shorter blue ribbon. They read:)

FREESTYLE SWIMMING
FIRST PLACE
(and)
1922

Mindy reloaded the camera several times in the ladies' room. She attempted to include everyone at the wake in at least one photograph. At a few minutes past eight, Tony, having recorded all the license plates in the parking lot, came into the building to observe first hand. He spotted two county detectives among the would-be mourners, nodded to both without speaking, and attempted to blend in, ignoring Mindy. By nine o'clock, all but just a few remained when one of the attendants announced that the funeral home was closing.

Tony approached the new widower, showed his credentials and introduced himself. To Tony's surprise, the man knew nothing of Tony or his meeting and/or phone calls with his late wife. She had apparently told him nothing.

"I met with her in the Star Diner several weeks back. She had responded to an ad that I ran warning former jurors of the Cassetti trial that they were in danger. I specifically urged her to have you contact me, and I advised her to spend the next few weeks with your daughter in Moscow,

THE CASE OF THE DEAD JURORS • 209

Pennsylvania."

"She never said a word to me. What's your name again?"

"Tony Donohoo. Here's my card. I have a request. The guest register in the foyer. Would you take a minute with your son and daughters to go over the names and check off anybody that you don't know?"

"What? Now?"

"Yes, now. While the four of you are here. It can't take five minutes. Please."

"What do you want it for?"

"Investigating. I have the guest registers for the other seven jurors who have been murdered. I want to compare handwriting for those guests that you don't know personally."

"What do you think? That the killer would walk in here and sign his name in the book?"

"Humor me, please."

"Is this gonna cost me anything?"

"Not a penny. The spouse of one of the other victims is my client. I'll get the register back to you in a week or so."

"So you don't think it's suicide?" asked Mr. Bankowski.

"I know it's not suicide. Your wife was murdered, without question."

"That ain't what the cops think."

"I can't help that. Do I get the book?"

"Okay, let me get my kids together to look through it."

* * *

From the funeral home, Tony and Mindy drove up the Seven Sisters hills to Englewood Cliffs for a drink at the Oasis. He parked behind the building in a gravel lot.

"It was like pulling teeth to get the register. If he hadn't finally agreed, I was about to tell him to stick it up his ass. Then I had to go all over it again for his kids. What could have taken five minutes took a half-hour."

"And if it's like the other sign-in books, it won't reveal a thing," said Mindy.

"Give me another Old Grand Dad on the rocks and a Seven and Seven for the lady." Tony said to the bartender.

THIRTY-SIX

Tony and Mindy exited the Oasis and walked to the car parked out back. Opening her door for her as she slid into the passenger seat, Mindy was glowing in the moonlight and Tony bent over to give her a kiss. At that instant he heard the crack of a pistol and a singing bullet sailing over his head.

"*On the floor!*" he shouted. Ducking, he pulled his own .38. The shots had come from somewhere behind him. The Oasis was separated from another tavern, Connolly's Cabin, by a patch of woods about fifty yards wide.

Tony heard the sound of someone thrashing through the woods. He got up from his crouch and with pistol in hand raced toward the woods, but couldn't see any one. He stopped once to listen. Hearing nothing, he advanced using the trees to act as cover.

He heard the cough of a car engine starting, and broke into a run toward Connolly's Cabin's tiny parking lot. All he could see was red taillights on a dark colored automobile accelerating up the road.

He hurried back to his own car. Mindy was standing outside the car on the side away from the woods.

"Did you see anybody?"

"No, are you all right?" Tony asked.

"I'm fine. What about you?"

"I'm good. Make a note of the time."

"I got five after ten," Mindy said scribbling in a notebook."

"Let's walk over to Connolly's and see what's what."

There were only three cars in Connolly's parking lot. The bartender, a comical old guy named Oscar, greeted Tony by name. Three customers sat at the bar.

"Oscar, did anyone leave within the last twenty minutes or so?" Tony asked.

"No, nobody left."

"There are three cars in the lot, but there are four of you here. Did somebody come with somebody else?"

"My wife dropped me off," said Oscar. "She'll be back before closing."

"So each of you three," Tony addressed the customers at the bar, "came in your own car.

What kind of car do you each drive and what color?"

"'48 tan Chevy."

"'49 Ford, green two-door."

"1950 black Olds sedan."

"Okay. Somebody followed us to the Oasis, but they parked in this lot. That was about half an hour ago. When we came out, the person fired a shot at me, then ran back here and drove off. Now, did any of you arrive here in the last thirty minutes?"

Two of the barflies said no. The third one said: "I got

here about fifteen minutes ago."

"And you said you had the black Olds. So when you got here how many cars were in the lot? Two or three? Think about it."

"Yeah, I think there was three."

"All right, close your eyes and try to let the picture come up. There was a tan '48 Chevy and a green '49 Ford. What was the third car?"

"It was parked over by the road, not near the entrance to the bar. I didn't really take notice."

"Was it dark or light colored?"

"Dark, I think."

"What about the size?"

"I don't know. Nothin' big like a Caddy or a Buick."

"Station wagon, convertible, sedan, coupe?"

"It wasn't a wagon or a convertible. I guess it was a sedan or a coupe. That's all I can tell you."

"Gimme change for the phone," said Tony tossing a dollar on the bar.

Tony dialed the number of the Ocean County Sheriff to report the shooting incident. The Borough of Englewood Cliffs had a police force of only five members. At this time of night, only one would be on duty patrolling the town. The sheriff's office would contact the on-duty cop by radio.

Tony and Mindy left the bar and returned to where his car was parked. Ten minutes later, a young officer showed up. Tony presented his credentials and told him what happened.

"Know anybody who's got a gripe?" asked the cop.

"It's hard to do my job without pissing somebody off. Right now I'm working a case that involves jurors from an old trial getting knocked off. It could have something to do with that."

"Oh yeah, I read about that in the papers. Got any idea what type of gun it was?"

"It was definitely a pistol."

"A .45?"

"No. It wasn't the sound of a .45. Some smaller caliber."

"And you didn't fire back?"

"Never saw anybody to fire at. I heard thrashing around from the woods. But I took my time in the woods listening and taking cover. Then I heard the car start, but as I told you, I didn't get a good look. It must have been parked in Connolly's lot. One of the customers said there was an extra car in the lot when he got there about 9:50, but all he could be certain of was that it was dark in color and was a sedan or coupe and not one of the big boys.

"Anyway, the bullet must have lodged in the rear wall of the Oasis. How about we find it and dig it out?"

"I'd rather leave that for the detectives," said the cop.

"Are you gonna stay here until the detectives arrive?" said Tony.

"No, of course not. I have to patrol."

"Then you're gonna leave the gate unlocked for the shooter to come back and remove the bullet?"

"I'll turn in a report. The Chief might want to talk to you."

"Here's my card. By the way, the chief investigator in

this juror case is Detective Al McGuirl, over at county. Please see that he's informed. Now we didn't quite clear this up. Are you gonna remove the bullet or not?"

"I'm not. I told you. I'll let the detectives do that."

"Then I'll do it."

"I can't let you do that," said the cop.

"As a commissioned New Jersey State Detective, not licensed but commissioned, I have police powers. If you're unwilling to remove the bullet, then I will. I prefer that you watch me do it, but I'm going to do it with or without you."

"Okay. You do it and I'll watch, but then I take the bullet into my custody to give to the detectives."

"Now we're communicating," said Tony. After searching for a minute or two, he found the hole in the wood siding and dug the bullet out with a pocket knife. It was a .38 slug. Tony studied it for a few moments and handed it to the cop.

"Okay. I'll hold this for the detectives. You take care now. You too, Miss," said the cop as he returned to the police cruiser.

"Mindy, stand in front of the hole. I'm going to get a read on where the shooter stood by lining up the passenger door of the car with you." Tony got a flashlight out of the car and cut off a piece of a rope he had in the trunk. He proceeded to walk into the woods and moved until he could see Mindy standing about thirty feet behind the car door. He moved tangentially, so as not to trod on the same ground where the shooter stood. He presumed the shooter would have been in the woods for cover, but not so deep as to obscure the target. He found a spot with a sapling that had a near horizontal branch about five and a half feet off the ground that would have made a perfect brace for the pistol. He saw some disturbance of flora but no discernible footprints. He leaned out and looped the rope over the branch to mark the spot for the detectives, who won't have Tony's car to use as a guide.

Tony returned to the car and got his camera out. He photographed the hole in the wall up close, and then took several pictures at various distances of the path the bullet must have traveled.

"Do you think whoever did this was trying to hit you?" asked Mindy.

"I heard that round whiz by. If I hadn't bent over to kiss you, I'd have a hole in my head right now. Thank God for raging hormones."

"So what do you feel like doing now? You want to come to my place?" Mindy asked.

"A bullet missing your head has a strange phenomenon. It drives sex well down the ladder of what's next. We have a stop to make."

"Where?"

"We got to check out someone's car."

THIRTY-SEVEN

Fifteen minutes later, Tony arrived at his destination. He parked down the street from the house he was interested in.

"Come on, Mindy, let's you and me take a little walk. It's been forty-five minutes since the shot was fired, but only about thirty minutes since the car got here."

They approached the house on foot. There was no garage and both cars were in the driveway. Tony walked up to the cars and placed his palm on one hood, which was cold to the touch, but the other was warm and the engine was making that ticking noise when it's cooling off.

Tony nodded to Mindy and she put her hand on the hood as well. She entered the time in her notebook. 10:51 P.M.

"Take a note of that decal, Mindy."

"Lodi Quality Used Cars," Mindy read off as she wrote it down.

* * *

Friday, November 6, 1953 - 10:30 A.M.

Tony drove out Route 46 to Lodi. There was a mile-long

strip of used car lots. Bare bulbs were strung everywhere for nighttime customers. He pulled into the Lodi Quality Used Cars lot. There was a '48 blue Buick convertible on a raised platform, shining like a new dime. The top was down and zebra skin seat covers were visible. The radio antenna wasn't the one the car came with. This one was a novelty item and looked like a miniature TV antenna, with horizontal attachments

"Could I see the manager, please," Tony said to a man who approached him when he entered the office.

"That's me, Jimmie Tubbiello. Here's my card."

"And here's mine," said Tony flashing his shield. "New Jersey State Detective. I hope you can help me out."

"Sure thing, if I can."

"You sold a car here a couple of months back. I'd like to speak to the salesman who made the deal."

"You got a problem?"

"Not with you. Not with him."

"Okay, who was the buyer?"

Tony gave the name.

"Well, that ain't hard. I don't even have to look it up. It was me."

"Oh, you remember it?"

"Yeah, the customer wanted a blue '50 - '51 Plymouth sedan. That was in maybe June or July. We didn't have one. The customer said to call if one came in. A few weeks later, I got a creampuff '48 in and I called. The customer asked if I didn't understand what I was told. A '50 or '51 and blue.

And then hung up. My brother-in-law works at another lot down the road. I told him the story and he had the same customer."

"What's his name and which lot does he work in?"

"Why? You wanna talk to him, too?"

"Yes, I do. What's his name and where does he work?

"Phil Carbone. He's at Bergen Auto Sales."

"Thank you. So what happened next?"

"Yeah, well, sometime in August, what comes in but a nice '51 blue job. I call and the customer is here within an hour with eleven hundred in cash. Didn't even haggle."

Thirty minutes later, Tony walked into Bergen Auto Sales and asked for Phil Carbone, who walked out with a big smile on his face probably figuring some one had referred him and a sale was in the works.

"Good morning, sir. Phil Carbone here. What can I do for you today?"

"Tony Donohoo, New Jersey State Detective." Carbone stared at Tony's shield and I.D. with something akin to alarm.

"What's this about?"

"Nothing for you to worry about. I talked to Jimmie Tubbiello, and he mentioned that you and he shared a prospective car purchaser a few months back." Tony mentioned the name and the request.

Carbone confirmed that he had called the customer with a green '50 Plymouth and gotten his head bitten off. He also confirmed the name of the customer which matched what his brother-in-law had told Tony.

* * *

"And you think I can get a search warrant on what you got. You're nuts, Donohoo," shouted Al McGuirl. "Just because ballistics matches up the slug from Haines' house with the one fired at you don't tell me who was holding the gun."

"As usual, McGuirl, you're not listening. I know who was holding the gun. And you don't have to actually get a search warrant, you just have to pretend you've got one.."

"I don't know. Give it to me again."

* * *

"Hello."

"May I speak to Mr. Haines, please," said Dolly Donohoo.

"He's not home right now. Who's calling?"

"Is this Mrs. Haines?"

"Yes, but I asked who's calling."

"I don't want to give my name. I work in the Bergen County Courthouse. I suppose I can talk to you. Your husband has always been nice to me, and I just don't think it's right what's happening."

"What are you talking about?"

"Well, Mr. Notella, the County Prosecutor, was in here with one of his detectives and they went to Judge Willcox to get a search warrant for your house. I know Mr. Haines is a nice man and I don't like to see him abused this way."

"When did this happen?"

"Just a few minutes ago."

"Did they get the warrant?"

"I can't be sure, but I think so. They left as if they had some place to go if you know what I mean."

"I'm sure it doesn't mean anything. After all, we have nothing to hide, but thank you for calling."

Dolly Donohoo replaced the phone in the cradle.

"That was great, Dolly," said Mindy. "You should have been an actress. I couldn't have done it myself because she might recognize my voice."

"She didn't seem overly concerned," said Dolly.

"We'll see about that."

* * *

Within two minutes of getting the call, Thais Haines was in her blue 1951 Plymouth and heading out of town. What she didn't know was that there were three unmarked police cars doing surveillance on her and followed along as she left the neighborhood in Maywood. Trailing along behind the police cars at a safe distance was Tony Donohoo in his '49 blue Ford.

Thais worked her way out to U.S. Route 4 and headed eastbound. She turned off for Kinderkamack Road and headed north. McGuirl in one car and two other detectives in their cars followed at a distance. Each detective would follow Thais for a short distance and then turn off to allay suspicion. Bringing up the rear end was Tony Donohoo. She traveled through River Edge, then Oradell and finally into Emerson. When she reached the Oradell Reservoir she pulled over and parked.

She got out and began to walk toward the water with her purse in her hand.

As she neared the water, she took an object out of the purse and the first police car closed in.

"Mrs. Haines! This is the police! Stand right where you are! Do not move!" The police loudspeaker's order echoed across the reservoir. But Thais Haines ignored the order and began to run and then flung an object toward the water. But it struck a tree branch and fell to the ground not more than two feet from the water's edge. The detectives were on her in no time. McGuirl picked up the gun, a .38 Smith and Wesson revolver, using a handkerchief and placed it in a paper bag.

"Mrs. Haines," intoned McGuirl, "you're under arrest."

"What's the charge?" she screamed, as one of the detectives slipped handcuffs on her hands behind her back.

"Carrying a concealed and unlicensed firearm," said McGuirl.

THIRTY-EIGHT

Monday, November 9, 2016 - 9:30 A.M. Office of Bergen County Prosecutor Louis Notella

"So fill me in," said Louis Notella. Present in the room were Tony, Mindy, Big Al McGuirl, and three other detectives.

"Ballistics," said McGuirl, "shows that the gun that Thais Haines was trying to toss into the reservoir was the weapon used to fire at Donohoo in Englewood Cliffs, and it was also the gun used to fire into Bob Haines' house on October 20th. As a result of that, we've arrested Bob Haines for filing a false police report, and upgraded the charge against Thais Haines to attempted murder of Donohoo. But that doesn't prove that she murdered Malina Bankowski or any of the jurors."

"I believe Malina Bankowski killed most of the jurors," Tony said. "But I think she was alarmed when she saw my ad in the paper indicating the Cassetti jurors were at risk. Then, when Judge Huber released the names of the jurors to Mr. Notella, she was notified by his office that she may be in danger, and that scared her off for good. They were working together, without doubt, from the start. Thais had promised her nobody would ever connect the murders. I should say they weren't working together so much as Malina Bankowski was working for Thais, who used and manipulated her. It probably started with a chance meeting, where Thais recognized Bankowski as the woman who broke into tears in the jury box, when Judge Willcox gave Cassetti the electric chair. Malina was Thais' murder weapon. I believe that Thais intended from the very beginning to do away with Malina when the seventh juror had been killed. She wound up doing that one herself when Malina balked. Then she got rid of the murder weapon: Malina Bankowski.

"Thais milked her for information," Tony continued. "getting the names of the other jurors and which ones voted to convict the first day. It came out that Malina Bankowski actually liked Marcy Cavanagh, who was the most capable person on the jury. She was intelligent, civil and respectful of the other jurors. A natural leader. And although she was not the chosen foreman, she actually filled that role more than Donald Nagle, who was the foreman. Thais figured out how important Marcy had been and selected her as the first victim. Marcy was a petite gal. Malina Bankowski was a big athletic woman, and a swimming champion. I have no doubt that Thais sent Bankowski up to Sunrise Lake to lay in wait for Marcy to swim out to the float, and then overpower her."

"Why did she keep the orange swimming cap," McGuirl asked.

"I'm sure that Malina thought nothing of it and never

even mentioned it to Thais."

"How do you know any of that? Not think it, but know it?" asked McGuirl, who was squirming. He clearly wasn't enjoying being in the dark with the County Prosecutor watching.

Tony gave McGuirl a big grin and took out a pack of Luckies and offered them around. McGuirl took one, Notella refused, and Tony lit them with his Zippo.

"Al, I thought you'd never ask," said Tony, motioning Mindy to take over.

"It's in the notes that Tony gave you," said Mindy. "I went to see Bob and Thais Haines several hours after Susan Ganley was found dead on the pretense of warning them that the killer struck again. "Mr. Notella, did your office notify Haines of the murder of Susan Ganley?" Mindy asked.

"Not my office. Me personally. I called Bob Haines at his office about four o'clock the afternoon it happened. I also called Judge Willcox. I had my staff call all the living jurors that could be reached. Some of them had gotten out of town, I believe."

"I got to the Haines house about seven o'clock the night of the murder," Mindy said, "and informed them. They pretended not to know about it. Then Thais Haines said something very revealing."

"What was it?" asked Notella.

"She said, and I quote exactly, 'That's the seven of them.' There were, of course, twelve jurors, and in our interviews we learned that seven of them voted to convict the first day. They were sequestered overnight and the next day, with pressure upon the remaining five, they brought in a unanimous verdict. Susan Ganley was the seventh to be murdered, and, according to her husband, voted to convict the first day. Now, how could anybody who was not one of the jurors know that? If the killer is not one of the jurors, there's only one other way and that is information gained from one of the jurors. Thais told Tony she kept notes during the trial about the jurors but never knew any of their names and merely referred to them by the numbers assigned to each. But Thais knew there were seven and only seven who voted to convict the first day."

"Miss McCall," asked Notella, "what about their pretending not to know about the Ganley killing?"

"When I informed them of the murder, Bob Haines said 'Oh my God.' Then later, as I was finishing up the interview, he expressed surprise that no attempt had been made on the life of Judge Willcox. I then commented that I was also very surprised no one had notified them. Neither of them spoke."

"Lemme ask you something, Donohoo," McGuirl said. "You said Thais killed Mrs. Bankowski. How do you think she got in and out without being seen?"

"She drove her car into the driveway, went in the house, and forced Malina Bankowski out the back door and into the garage, probably at gunpoint, which couldn't have been observed by anyone who was not in the back yard. Then she handcuffed her to the bumper and started Bankowski's '52 blue Plymouth, and left. She got into her own car and drove away."

"She'd risk someone seeing her car in the driveway? Doesn't make sense," said McGuirl.

"She drove a 1951 blue Plymouth sedan. Bankowski's was a '52 blue Plymouth. The difference between a '51 and a '52 is maybe the windshield wipers are an inch longer. The vehicles were virtually identical. Certainly so to a casual observer. Furthermore, she bought that car months ago with intention to use it for that purpose."

"How do you know that?" asked Notella.

"Because she started looking for that car two months before she bought it. She went to at least two used car lots in Lodi and told them she wanted a blue Plymouth from 1950 to 1952. There were no significant exterior changes during those years. When the salesman called her once and told her he had gotten in a real nice '48 Plymouth, she got angry with him and repeated the original demand, and then hung up. She did the same thing with another salesman, who worked at a different lot. I interviewed that guy also, and it was the same story. He called her to say he'd gotten a '51 Plymouth sedan in, but it was green. She asked him why he couldn't understand the car had to be blue and hung up on him.

"In addition, both the Bankowski woman and Thais are - or were - large women. 5-8, 5-9, and 160 pounds or more. Mrs. Bankowski often wore kerchiefs on her head. I have no doubt that Thais wore a kerchief and a green coat, like Bankowski, and arrived in a virtually identical car. The neighbor across the street saw her arrive and naturally assumed it was Bankowski. When you search the Haines' house, I strongly suspect you'll find a green woman's coat."

"Supposing' Bankowski's car was in the driveway instead of the garage, what then?" asked McGuirl.

"I asked Stanley Bankowski about his late wife's habit in putting the car in the garage. He said she put the Plymouth in the garage every night. Hers was the newer car. His went in the driveway. He said that if she used the car and expected to take it out again that day, she would leave it in the driveway So, the car may very well have been in the driveway on former days, and in that case, Thais would have driven right on by and try again another day."

"Why are you so sure that Thais and Mrs. Bankowski were in a conspiracy from the beginning?" asked Notella.

"If Malina Bankowski were to pick the first victim, it would have been Judge Willcox, not Marcy Cavanagh. If Malina had independently decided to commit murder, I think there would have been just one: Judge Willcox. Malina, who wasn't very bright and who I think was a little bit crazy, was angriest at the judge, but no attempt was ever made on his life, because Thais wasn't interested in taking revenge on Willcox."

"Why not?" asked Notella.

"Because Thais didn't give a fat rat's ass about the life of Harry Cassetti," Tony said. " She was out to get even with what she called the morons who convicted on circumstantial evidence, and in her opinion, ruined her husband's career. Not only did he get passed over for the judgeship, but he got bad press for his incompetent defense of Cassetti. Thais probably told Malina that they would get Judge Willcox

The Case of the Dead Jurors • 229

last, just to appease her."

"I think you put forward a very compelling case, Mr. Donohoo, and I have to commend you and Miss McCall for your diligence and professionalism. I also have to say there is a lot of conjecture in all that you've said. I don't think I could get a conviction on that evidence, or lack of it," said Notella.

"Al," said Tony, "Do you have the lineup scheduled?"

"Yeah, but you didn't tell me who the witness is."

"Surprise, surprise. Let's go down and see what we will see," said Tony. "Mr. Notella, I think you might find this interesting."

* * *

Ten minutes later, Tony and Mindy met Patrick Ganley in the lobby.

"How are your kids dealing with the loss of their mother?" Mindy asked.

"They took it hard, but I'm hoping in time they get past it."

"And how are you doing?"

"I'm still kicking myself in the ass, if you want to know. But what's going on? What am I doing here? What do they want?" asked Ganley.

"You'll find out. I don't want to put anything in your mind. But let me ask you something.

Before we go back there, did you ever hear anything about the fingerprints on that ten dollar bill?" Tony asked. "I couldn't ask McGuirl because I wasn't supposed to know about it."

"Yeah. McGuirl said they could read mine but the others were smudged. They couldn't get anything usable."

Mindy then took Patrick Ganley by the arm and escorted him back to the viewing room, with Tony taking up the rear. The three of them, along with Notella and McGuirl, entered the darkened booth and looked through the one-way glass at the raised platform.

"Sergeant, bring in the women," said Notella over the microphone. Voices from the booth could only be heard when the microphone was buttoned. Five women walked out under the orders of the police sergeant. Each had a small placard hanging over her chest with a number from one through five. Thais Haines wore number four.

"Mr. Ganley, have you ever seen any of these women before?" Notella asked.

Everyone watched realization creep across Ganley's features. His mouth fell open, but he didn't speak.

"Mr. Ganley," said Notella, after several moments passed, "have you—"

"You bet your sweet ass I have." Ganley finally said. "Number four."

"And where and under what circumstances did you see number four?"

"A pound of Kielbasi and a half-pound of swiss cheese," replied Ganley.

THIRTY-NINE

Thursday, November 19, 1953, 7:30 P.M.—The Emerson Hotel, Emerson, New Jersey.

"I'm delighted you two could join me for dinner," said Lou Notella, who had risen from a table. "You'll see it in Saturday's paper because I'm giving a press conference tomorrow. But I wanted you both to know what has happened."

"You're giving a press conference before the trial? Isn't that a bit unusual?" asked Tony.

"There isn't going to be a trial. Thais has confessed. How about a drink?" The waiter had approached. Tony and Mindy both ordered dry martinis. Lou asked for a refill on his Cutty Sark and soda.

"What exactly did she confess to?" Mindy asked.

"She confessed to the murders of Susan Ganley and Malina Bankowski, and to the attempted murder of Tony. Oh, and she cleared up one little question that I had floating around in my mind. I couldn't figure out why Thais didn't leave Ganley's Deli by the back door, which is the way she came in. She said that after she had knifed Susan Ganley, she walked out to the front of the store to empty the cash register to make it look like robbery. But at that moment, Pat Ganley walked across the street and she only had time to get around the counter and pretend to be a customer."

"Yeah...I thought of that too, but kinda forgot about it. Why do you think she confessed? Did you have to make any concessions?" Tony said.

"Life on each count of murder. Twenty years on the attempted. All three to be served concurrently. With good behavior, she'll probably be out in twenty-five years. She'll be in her sixties by then."

"No charges for conspiracy with Bankowski? Accessory before the fact?" Tony queried.

"It never would have stuck. Our case was weak. We know she did it but proving it to a jury would be difficult and might even screw up the murder case."

"So she confessed to take the death penalty off the table." Mindy said.

"Does the name Margaret Meierhoffe mean anything to either of you?" Notella asked. Both Tony and Mindy shook their heads.

"Margaret Meierhoffe was the last woman executed in New Jersey. 1881. She murdered her husband. In those days, the death penalty was hanging. There was no way I was going to seek the death penalty, especially for a woman. I'm not a big fan of the death penalty, and I wasn't even before the Cassetti trial.

"I don't agree that it is a deterrent, unless you count the next time. If you're dead, you don't get to kill anybody else.

I was shocked when Willcox sentenced Cassetti to the chair. I never asked for it. He alone has to carry that rock around for the rest of his life. Some people argue that the state has to bear the expense of keeping the convicted in prison for all those years, but that's only because they don't know what it costs for a trial and appeals. And then there is the ugly spectacle of the state taking a life and the effect that has.

"Anyway, we cut a deal with Thais and her lawyer. So neither of you will have to testify."

The waiter reappeared, everybody ordered the house specialty—sirloin steak, medium-rare—and another round of drinks.

"Did you see any involvement Bob Haines might have had in the conspiracy for any of the murders?" Tony asked.

"No. There was nothing that indicated that. Haines married a mother figure. I can see him going home and sitting on the edge of the bed and whining about his day to Mommie. And she would comfort him and build him up. When he lost the shot at becoming a judge, she was incensed. The funny thing was that in our negotiations, she didn't seem to have any problem with me. Some say people can't understand why a lawyer will represent bad guys. They don't think it through. But Thais thought like a lawyer, so Willcox and I were okay. Anyway, Haines was in the clear except for that false police report. But I can tell you one thing. I'm glad the sonofabitch never became a judge. The story that went around was that Thais had family connections. Her aunt and uncle pulled some strings and laid out some cash to get him considered in the first place. Big Republicans over in Cresskill, name of Magee."

"I've met the dowager queen," said Tony. "Interviewed her. She wasn't helpful."

"Christ, Donohoo, you do get around, don't you?"

"So what are you gonna tell the reporters about who did the first six murders?" Mindy asked.

"I'm going to let them infer that Thais did those too, but that it would be a cleaner process with just charging her for the last two. I'll let them think we can always go back and try her for any or all of the first six if something goes awry."

"And you're not going to tell them it was Malina Bankowski?" Tony said.

"What would be the point? She already got the death penalty. Besides, if we did that we'd still have to prove it in civil court if her family brought an action for slandering the memory of a wife and mother. She's dead. Let her stay dead. One thing I wanted to ask was how you knew that Thais was the lady in the deli."

Before answering, Tony pulled a Lucky out of his pack and tapped the end on the table before lighting it.

"I had taken pictures of all the living jurors that I interviewed and got others from the surviving spouses. I used them as memory aids because most people wouldn't remember their fellow jurors' names but would recognize them in a photo. When I met with Patrick Ganley, I showed him the photos and he didn't know any of them...including Malina Bankowski. So I knew it wasn't her in the deli. McGuirl put out an appeal for the lady but got nothing. That's not conclusive but I was pretty sure the lady wasn't just a customer.

Ganley had never seen her before, and he strikes me as someone with a good memory for that sort of thing. Despite that, she knew him because when he walked into the store she asked him for service. If she was a first time customer, she would have assumed he was a customer also, not an employee of the deli. When Mindy and I interviewed Ed Gleason, he said he recognized Thais from a newspaper picture taken the day of the trial back in '47. It hit me that I didn't have a picture of Thais Haines. Therefore, Ganley hadn't seen her photo. When he came in to look over the lineup, I was ninety, maybe ninety-five percent sure that he'd pick out Thais. He did."

"You make it sound simple," said Notella. "I'm really impressed on your handling of this case. Without you, it may never have been closed. It's a classic example of how jurisdictional matters can be counter-productive. Christ, there were six murders each being treated as accidental death before they were connected. You're the one, Tony, that figured that out."

"Actually, it was Brendan Cavanagh. And he did it with only two deaths."

"By the way," said Mindy, "if you ever had any qualms about steering me to O'Neill's Bar and Grill and Andy Panzavecchia, you should know that you almost saved the life of Charlie Jenkins. You would have if he wasn't such a dumb bastard. Tell him, Tony."

"Andy gave me the lead on one of the jurors being an auto salesman in Englewood but couldn't remember the guy's name. I hit all the dealers and finally came face to face with Jenkins. But he played it cagey with me and wouldn't admit to being one of the former jurors. The very next night he was murdered."

Notella grinned. "I don't know what you're talking about, Mindy. I just thought it would be a nice place to have a drink after work. But I had still another reason to meet with you. I want to offer you both jobs as investigators on the prosecutor's staff."

"As for me, thanks, but no thanks. Mindy is free to go her own way."

"I'm not cut out for government work, so I will pass also. But, it's nice to be be asked," said Mindy. "Anything else?"

As the steaks were being served, Notella said: "When I give the press conference, you two are getting full credit for solving this case. It will piss off Big Al McGuirl no end, and that's all the more fun. Now let's eat."

About the Author

Rod Sterling was born and raised in New Jersey. During his senior year in High School he joined the Air Force and spent a year in Texas and three years deployed in France, England, and Tripoli. Rod took over the family business—a saloon—after a fire had seriously injured his father. Although he sold the business a few years later, he ownership in three more bars: Manhattan's east side, Fort Lee, N.J., and St. Thomas, U.S. Virgin Islands.

After leaving the saloon business, Rod was a private detective in New Jersey and New York. As a young father, he went into real estate and eventually owned a multi-office chain of offices. Retiring 25 years later, Rod served as mayor in Ocean County, New Jersey. He now lives in Virginia and draws on his vast experience as inspiration for his novels. *The Case of the Dead Jurors* is his fourth published mystery.